# THE RAIN TREE

# THE RAIN TREE

## Will Cook

GUNSMOKE

This hardback edition 2010
by BBC Audiobooks Ltd
by arrangement with
Golden West Literary Agency

ISBN 978 1 408 46296 6

British Library Cataloguing in Publication Data available.

Printed and bound in Great Britain by
CPI Antony Rowe, Chippenham and Eastbourne

# THE RAIN TREE

# Chapter One

Jennifer Martin had to clutch tightly her son's arm to keep him from dashing outside and joining his father. She held him facing her, near the kitchen table, and she tried to brush some order into his hair. Dipping the brush into a pan of water, she soaked the hair and swept it back, then watched it stubbornly pop up again.

Outside Jim Martin fired another shot, the full boom big and hollow sounding. Tad squirmed, and his mother rapped him lightly with the back side of the hair brush, not hard enough to hurt him but hard enough to let him know she meant business.

"Awwww, Mom," Tad said. "Whatcha fussin' for? It'll dry out in ten minutes."

"I know that, but it's a proper start that counts." She gave the brush a final flick through the hair, then released him. "Go tell your father we're ready and ask him how much longer he's going to shoot off that silly cannon."

Jim Martin was standing with his hands on his hips, head tipped back, looking at a cloudless, glass-bright sky. He heard the boy come up and said: "Maybe I ought to fire another one. What do you think?"

"Mom's ready, Pa."

"Hmm," Martin said, "I guess the atmosphere ain't right, or somethin'. If that Chinese powder gets in from San Francisco, I might have better luck. From what I hear, they get rain with it."

Jim Martin was a square-bodied man, lank in the arms and quite tall when standing for he had unusually long legs. He had never owned a pair of jeans that fit him properly. When they were right at the waist, they were always six inches short in the legs. His face was dark, and his hair was dark, and there was never any non-sense in his expression. Quite early in life he had learned that living was no joke. He was a solemn man but not humorless, for he joked with the boy and his wife, but to all others he presented as unchanging a stoicism as the land on which he lived.

"One of these days I'm going to try fire," Jim Martin said. "They say it'll bring rain because it's the opposite of water."

"Who's they, Pa?"

"Hmm?" He looked at Tad. "Oh, people who know about those things. Rainmaking's pretty complicated, son. There's a lot of ways for a man to get rain. The trouble is, I just haven't hit on one yet." Then he put his arm around the boy's shoulders and walked with him to the house.

When judged by itself, Martin did not have much of a place — just a three-room, unpainted, clapboard house, a barn, and a small horse corral sitting in the middle of eight thousand very dry acres. Yet his position, his possessions were average in a country that was long on land and short on water.

Jennifer came out, her step stirring some loose planks in the porch floor. She was a chunky woman, round faced, full lipped, and she wore a dress that was too tight for her, not because she wanted to but because it was seven years old and had been let out to the limit. She wore a wide hat to shield her face from the strong sun and a pair of gloves to cover the work roughness of her hands.

"Are you going to take the cannon back?" she asked.

"I thought I'd wait until I got that Chinese powder," Jim Martin said.

She looked at him and smiled and shook her head, for she considered his efforts to bring rain a little foolish, but she would not chide him for trying or talk against his notions. She believed that a man's foolishness had to run a proper course, and the quicker the better.

"Jim, the cannon belongs on the courthouse lawn, not in back of the barn."

"Well, they didn't put a time limit on my borrowin' it," he said. Then he turned to the boy. "Fetch the wagon, Tad. Your ma's in an impatient mood." There was a hint of teasing in his voice, and he winked at the boy before he dashed to the barn.

"I've just got to get that boy a new pair of pants," Jennifer said. "You could use a new pair too, Jim. How much is this Chinese powder going to cost?"

"Hmm, I guess a few dollars. Not much."

He was being vague with her, but she did not make an issue of it. Tad brought the wagon to the porch, and Martin boosted her onto the seat, then took the reins, and drove out of the yard.

The road ran across so vast an expanse of flatlands that young Tad could not imagine what it was like on either side. He sat in the bed of the wagon, his feet dangling over the back, his bare legs powdered by the dust raised from the wheels. Tad liked to look back on things, for he was nine years old, life was both new and old, and one day was pretty much the same as the one before, although he always woke up hoping it would be different. For a time he watched the dust raised by the iron-shod wheels. It was deeper than the rim so that, when the wheels turned, a little of it was lifted on each spoke, and then it fell like brown water.

This was autumn, and the grass was withered under the pitiless sun. The dust was powder on his clothes and ground into the pores of his skin and in the food, so that everything tasted gritty. He amused himself by humming with his mouth open, a steady, *"Aaaaaaa-aaaaaaa,"* and the jolting wagon turned it into a vibrato. He was a thin boy with his father's dark hair and eyes that seemed too big for his face. He wore a pair of faded overalls and nothing else. Each spring and fall he got a new pair, and by summer the knees were beyond patching, so his mother cut them off, which took care of the wearing and growing. For the winter months he got a pair of brass-eyelet shoes, a shirt, and a coat. These were worn out by spring.

He had his work, and he had his fun, and a lot of times it was sort of run in together, like going the six miles to Plumb Creek for water once a week. They had to haul it in barrels, and that was work, but his father always let him play in the creek when they got there, and that was fun.

Jim Martin turned his head and said: "You still comin' back there?"

"Yep," Tad said. He looked at his father for a moment, and both of them smiled, then Jim Martin turned back to his driving.

Jennifer observed them both for a moment, catching this subtle fun play that seemed to go on continually between father and son. Looking out over the sweaty backs of the team, she studied the road ahead, straight as a man could make it, a groove in the earth, leading

10

blindly toward distant hills. The sun was intense, and heat bounced from the road, and the dust raised by the wheels mingled with the sweat on her face until her skin felt muddy to the touch. She kept looking ahead, studying those hills as she had a thousand times and wondering what had made her husband stop on the waterless flats when a little more effort would have carried him on to something else — something better than he had. Then she supposed all women thought like that, always believing that they had missed out on something better. A good man, a steady man like Jim Martin, made do with what he had and didn't stand around whining about what he had missed.

Martin was not yet thirty. She was four years younger, and she supposed they were both quite young to have a nine-year-old boy, but then they were the kind who made their big mistakes early in life. He had been nineteen that year she became pregnant, and he had made the long journey from Texas to Kansas and back with all the hell in between, not knowing she was pregnant. A week before the baby was due, he arrived home, then rode forty miles to Tyler to get a Mexican priest so the boy would have a name.

Jennifer Martin never entertained a moment's doubt that he loved her, and they never talked about those empty, lonesome, hopeless months that she waited. But she knew that he thought of them often, for he seemed sorry to have been young and thoughtless, and in many small ways he tried to make up for this.

From the side of the road a flock of sage hens rose with a whir and beating of wings, and Jim Martin turned his head to watch them fly off a way then settle in the withered grass again.

11

Tad said: "If you'd had your shotgun, Pa, you could have got 'em."

"Who'd want to kill a skinny bird?" He shook his head. "Hardly enough grass left standing for them to take cover."

To his left and away from the road thin, bony cattle wandered and grazed, walking off as many pounds as they put on. They wore Martin's brand, the M Cross, and he stopped the wagon to have a look. He expected them to be on that side of the road, for Fred Sales's creek lay in that direction, and the creek was the only decent bit of water on Martin's place, save for a piddling seep in the north section.

"When I see those poor cattle," Jennifer said, "I don't care how much you spend on rainmaking gimcracks."

"Five inches would bring the grass back," Martin said. "Five inches of water would put money pounds on those steers." Then he sighed and clucked the team into motion. "Thank God I shipped in the spring, or we'd be stone broke."

In the distance he could see trees rising from the flatlands, a dark smudge, for they were still some miles away. There was water there, and a town, and a break in the monotony of so much flat land. There were times when Jim Martin's eyes got tired of looking at so great a distance. It seemed that he would get so used to focusing his attention to limitless miles that, when he went to town and saw everything close up, his vision would blur a little.

They arrived in town early in the afternoon. It was a four-hour drive from their place. Martin always stopped just as he reached the end of the street for there were trees and shade, and he pulled to the side of the road, feeling the coolness on his head and shoulders. Birds rustled among the branches, talking to each other, and somewhere down the street a songbird trilled and flew from limb to limb.

Martin got down from the wagon, tied the team, then helped his wife to the ground. Tad scuffed his feet in the dust by the hitching rack, then went over to the boardwalk and squatted to study the many bird droppings there.

"You keep out of that," Jennifer said. "Play nice and, if you play with town kids, don't fight. And say your howdy to your elders."

"Yes, Ma."

"I think I'll go on to the hotel and freshen up a bit," Jennifer said. "I'll meet you at the store?"

"Yes," Martin said. Then he bent and quickly kissed her, and color came into her round cheeks and a deep pleasure in her eyes.

"Why, Jim! On the street?"

"That's my brand," he said, smiling.

He watched her walk away, then he stood there and looked at the town. The main street had a long jog in it as though the people who laid it out had nearly changed their minds about its direction. It was a wide street, flanked by frame buildings and mud buildings. One looked as badly as the other. The hot winds off the flats had dried the wood until the edges of the boards curled, and nails were pulled. Then, during the brief winter rains, the boards swelled again and, if a man thought of it, he could take a hammer and drive all the nails back in again. With the adobe you just waited until the rains softened the outside quarter inch, then you patched the cracks with more mud; finally the walls

13

looked like an old varnished table, all minute cracks and wrinkles.

By observing the horses and buggies along the street, Jim Martin knew who was in town. He saw Fred Sales's rig parked in front of the cattle buyer's office, and this reminded Martin again that he'd have to talk to Sales about water.

"Come on, Tad," he said and walked slowly down the street, the boy padding along beside him. Martin's face was a study of neutrality, and there was a lot of it in his voice when he spoke again. "Tad, there's some people who don't understand a man who tries to make rain, so whatever's said, just pass it over. No more fights about it, you understand?"

"That Pete Goddard said you was soft in the head. That's why I fought."

Martin frowned. "Never you mind what he said. He's a chip off the old man, and Charlie Goddard is mean enough as it is. You just do what I say and don't bring any shame on your mother. The last time she had to apologize for you."

"Yes, Pa."

At the watering trough Martin stopped, picked Tad up by his overalls, and dumped him in the water. Then he set him on the sidewalk, and they both laughed. "Some way to cool off, huh?" Martin said.

"You said it!"

"Hmm, well, you'll never be pretty," Martin said, "but no one can say you ain't clean." He gave the boy a slap on the rump and sent him off. "Remember what I said now!"

Then he took off his hat and flogged great clouds of dust from his clothes, rolled his shirt sleeves, and plunged his head into the water. He blew bubbles and splashed and, when he stood erect, a tall, rail-thin man was walking toward him. He wore a thin cotton shirt, a pistol, and a badge was pinned over the left breast pocket. Martin shook the water from his hair like a dog shakes, then dried his eyes with a bandanna.

"Why didn't you sit in it?" the man asked.

Martin looked at Cal McKitrich and laughed. "Thought of it, but it's something only a boy could get away with." He put his bandanna away and rolled down the sleeves of his shirt. "Don't anything change around here?"

"The temperature," McKitrich said. "In the morning it's hot. In the afternoon it's hotter." He cocked a foot on the edge of the trough and leaned on his raised knee. "I was talking to Fred Sales. He said he heard you shootin' again, just as he was leaving for town." McKitrich smiled behind his thick mustache. "Jim, don't you mind being laughed at?"

"It ain't hurt me none," Martin said. He nodded toward the horses down the street. "Charlie Goddard come in?"

"Yeah, he's over to the saloon, lapping it up. When it gets late enough and his wife gets disgusted enough, she'll get someone to tie him on his horse and take him home. And next week, when it gets time to come to town, she'll pretend it never happened." McKitrich sighed heavily. "Jim, what makes people fool themselves? Charlie's wife pretends she's got the finest man in the world, and you shoot cannons off and fly kites and other damned things, thinking you'll get rain."

"I may get rain," Martin said firmly. "A man can have the gift, you know. It just takes time to develop it."

McKitrich knew better than genuinely to argue. He rolled a smoke, then passed the makings to Martin.

"Well, you know I wish you luck, Jim. But do me a favor, huh? When Charlie Goddard mentions some other hare-brained scheme to shoot water from the sky, ignore him, will you?"

"Because he's making fun of me?" Martin shook his head slowly. "Cal, sometimes fools come up with the truth. And I've always considered Charlie a real damned fool." He smiled then. "See you around."

"Jim!" Martin stopped and looked around. "Jim, did you really order some Chinese powder from San Francisco?"

"Yes," Martin said. "And I hope it's in."

He walked on down the street to the hotel porch where the ladies always gathered to talk and observe the happenings in the town. A small shaggy-haired dog lay beneath the lip of the boardwalk, where there was both shade and safety from being stepped on. Martin looked at the animal and thought of Tad. The boy ought to have a dog for a companion.

"I've never seen this dog before," he said to no one in particular.

Charlie Goddard's wife had been whispering something to Edith Sales. She stopped whispering and looked at Martin, then at the dog, as though she were comparing them in her mind and not finding much difference between them. "My boy was playing with him," she said. "He's a stray."

"Hmm," Jim Martin said. He turned then and faced the ladies. "I expect it'll get cooler this evening. We need a little rest from the heat."

"Last night was hot," Edith Sales said. She was not much older than Martin. Sales had been a middle-aged man when he married her. She was small and thin, and her hair had once been brown, but the sun had taken the color from it, leaving it pale and brittle. She wore it in a bun on the back of her head, braided, rolled, and pinned tightly.

"When you get some of that rain," Bess Goddard said, "send some our way. Edith says you've been shooting again."

They were laughing at him, and Martin glanced at his wife, feeling some shame because she had to endure this in silent embarrassment. Yet he said seriously: "I tried a dozen shots, yes. It's been in my mind that there's some combination of numbers to be used." He shook his head sadly. "But as yet I haven't hit on it."

"Jim," Jennifer said, "you haven't had your drink yet."

"Hmm," he said. She was reminding him in her way to go with the men. There he was not weaponless.

As he turned to cross the street, Charlie Goddard came out of Herb Manners's Saloon and had a quick look up and down the street. He saw Martin and stared for a moment, then he saw the dog. He squatted and snapped his fingers and whistled, and the dog, hungry for a friend, trotted across the street. Goddard laughed and scooped the dog in his arms and went back into the saloon.

Two more rigs came down the street, other families coming in for the weekly shopping and talk. Martin watched them get down and tie up, waved at them, then walked across to the saloon. He pushed inside. A small crowd stood at the bar, and they all turned their heads together and looked at him. The man next to Fred Sales moved aside slightly, making room for Martin. The place was hot and rank with the odor of soiled sawdust and cigar smoke. While Martin waited for Herb Manners to pour his drink, he listened to the beams in the ceiling shrink and pop.

Fred Sales said: "The poppin's about over. Rain next month."

From farther down Charlie Goddard said: "If Jim don't shoot us up a storm."

A few men laughed but not very much. Goddard grinned and held the shaggy dog by the scruff of the neck. The animal looked at Jim Martin, and Martin looked at the dog, and for a moment he thought he could communicate with the dog, so clear was the misery in the dog's eyes. The dog had made a mistake, thinking he had found a friend. Now he was sorry he had made the mistake, but like everyone else he wasn't sure what to do about it.

Sales pushed Martin's whiskey toward him, and Martin raised it. He studied the color of the whiskey then tossed it up to his lips, and afterward he stood there, holding it in his mouth as though letting the taste of it soak through him before he swallowed it. A timber in the roof creaked, and Martin set the empty glass on the bar. "You'd think it'd get dried out, wouldn't you?"

"Never quite dry enough," Sales said, "and never wet enough." Sales was a large man, heavily mustached and thick through the jaw. He frowned a great deal and worried a great deal, and he had a face full of wrinkles to prove it.

The room was very silent. A few botflies pestered the beer taps, and finally Herb Manners turned around and slapped at them with his towel. They buzzed away, circled, then came right back. He looked at them for a moment then said: "Lansing was in last week. It's dry all the way to the hills."

"I smelled rain a couple of weeks ago," one man said.

Everyone turned their heads and looked at him questioningly. They waited for him to say something else and, when he didn't, they all turned their heads back and looked into the dusty back-bar mirror.

"That must have been when Jim was flying his kites," Goddard said, grinning. "Huh, Jim?"

"I wonder if you'd laugh had it rained?" Martin said. He turned to Charlie Goddard. "Men make rain. Understand that?"

"Shhhure they do," Goddard said, nudging the man next to him.

Goddard was not a big man, not much more than five-foot three in his boots, but he had thick arms and a short upper body and a temper that most men respected. Goddard took the small man's attitude that, because he was small, he was entitled to pick up a brick to defend himself. He had never heard of rules for anything, and he liked to make his own and liked better making other men live by them.

"Plumb Creek has never been this low," Fred Sales said, thinking to turn the topic a little. "You notice that when you go after water, Jim?"

"Yes, and I've been careful not to muddy it." He knew Sales, knew that he was leading into something, something Martin did not want to hear, yet he would have to stand there and listen to Sales say it.

"You want another drink?" Sales asked. Martin nodded his head. "I think I'll have another, Herb." He pushed his glass toward the bartender. While the bottle was being tipped, Sales said: "Jim, I'm going to have to ask you to stop using so much water from my creek. Can't rightly stop your cattle from drinking, but two barrels a week is a lot, figurin' it on the long rule." He cast a sidelong glance at Martin. "You ain't sore, are you, Jim?"

"Why should he be sore?" Goddard asked. He pushed a man aside and came up to Martin, standing on his left side. "Hell, ain't Jim going to shoot himself up a storm when that Chinese powder gets here?"

"Why don't you shut up?" Sales asked bluntly. He spoke before thinking and regretted it, for Goddard's face settled into still, half-angry lines.

Martin sensed Sales's mistake and, when Goddard started to step past him, Martin raised an elbow quickly and jabbed Goddard in the pit of the stomach. The jolt caught him completely unprepared, and Goddard said: "*Uuuuuffffff!*"

"Say, I sure am sorry," Martin said soothingly. "Didn't hurt you now, did I, Charlie?"

Goddard looked at Martin for a long moment, then at Fred Sales. He turned back to the bar and snapped his fingers. "Give me another whiskey, Herb." To Sales he said: "I don't like to be talked sharp to, you understand?"

"Sure, Charlie. And I don't like people butting in when I'm telling a man he's through." He touched Jim Martin on the arm. "Jim, if we'd only get an early rain, things would change. But a man can't count on that any more."

Martin nodded. "The place was a dust patch when I bought it. That's why I got it so cheap." His shoulders rose and fell. "I've used too much of your water already, Fred. There ain't many men who'd do for me what you've done."

"Wish I could do more," Sales said. "That's the truth, Jim."

A man farther down the bar said: "Charlie, ain't you goin' to tell Jim about that rainmaker you heard about?"

20

Goddard sulked for a moment, trying to make up his mind. Martin turned to him, very serious. "If you know a man, Charlie, you ought to tell me." He watched Goddard's expression carefully, knowing as he had known before that probably it was a lie, something Goddard had cooked up as a joke. Still Jim Martin went along with it, thinking that any chance was better than none.

"Awww, it ain't much," Goddard said. "There's this old man over in Rock Springs who got water."

"Who in Rock Springs?"

"Patchin," Goddard said.

"I know that old man," Fred Sales said. "Charlie, you're talkin' through your hat. Jim, don't believe him."

"Go on," Martin said. "I want to hear about him." He looked at the others. "Any of you know about him?"

"I heard he was a witch," Herb Manners said. "You know, a water witch. He's brought in a couple of wells."

"He gets rain, too," Goddard said.

"Now, god damn it," Sales said, "this has gone far enough. These rainmakers are all fakes. No offense, Jim, but it's true."

"Then suppose you tell me," Goddard said, "just how come you're always runnin' over to Jim's place every time he flies a kite or somethin', huh? You don't believe none of this stuff, but you sure get your nose in there when anything's goin' on, don't you?"

"I have a normal man's curiosity," Sales said. "And I have an open mind. I'm ready to be shown a thing or two. Which is more than I can say for some in this room. But that's not the point now, Charlie, so don't try to sidetrack me. How many wells did this man, Patchin, witch for before one came in? No, I don't hold much faith

21

in those stories. You remember three years ago when I tried to get water in that seep I had? Cost me four hundred for the driller and rig, and at ninety feet we hit slate. The land's dry. God made it dry, and we got to live on it dry."

"If this man's got somethin' I haven't tried," Martin said, "I want to know about it."

"When God wants it wet," Sales said, "He makes it rain. And He frowns on men who try to take matters out of His hands."

"Now Fred, you're speakin' for God," Charlie Goddard said. "This fella's over in Rock Springs, Jim. Maybe it would be worth your while to go see him."

"Maybe it would be," Martin said softly. Then he looked at Charlie Goddard and smiled. "But promise me one thing, Charlie. Promise me the first look at your god-damned face if your lies turn out to be the truth." He took out a quarter and dropped it on the bar, then he went out and across the street to where his wife waited.

Each week Jim Martin and his wife and boy ate an early supper in the hotel dining room. It was a luxury he could not really afford, yet he always insisted on this extravagance. It was his way, he supposed, of showing her that she was not a prisoner to four walls, an eternally dusty house, and a dry land.

The boy came in just as they sat down. He knew not to be late. Taking his chair and tucking his napkin in the bib of his overalls, Tad said: "Can I have pie for dessert, Pa?"

Martin ran his fingers through his son's hair, trying to put some order to it. "All right, but eat slowly and chew each mouthful good."

The waiter brought them coffee, and Jim Martin gave

the boy half a cup. Jennifer fanned herself with a limp hand. "It must be a hundred and five in here," she said.

"Some day," Martin said, "I'm going to buy a thermometer and try to get up nerve enough to look at it." He paused before adding: "I saw Fred Sales. He wants me to use less water from the creek."

Jennifer frowned. "Jim, we need two barrels a week, with washing and all."

Martin nodded and glanced at the boy, who sat there, his attention fixed, listening, understanding completely the seriousness of what was being said. This saddened Martin, who believed that nine-year-old boys ought to be thinking about the crawdad holes and the rabbit runs and not paying any attention to whether their folks were going to be wiped out or not.

"In the saloon there was talk about a man in Rock Springs who gets water," he said. When he looked at her, he found her regarding him solemnly, much the same way she had regarded him when he talked about the kite flying and the Chinese powder. "Well, it wouldn't hurt to look into it, would it?"

"Did Charlie Goddard tell you this?"

"Yes," he said. "I know, he was pokin' fun at me. But what if he . . . ?" Martin shook his head. "I'll not go if you want it that way."

"It's not what I want," she said. "Jim, is it so hard to give up? To admit you've been licked?" She spread her hands briefly. "The land is bone dry. We all know that. We can't really change that." Reaching across the table, she took his right hand in hers. "Jim, sometimes it frightens me, the way you go at a thing. Day after day shooting the cannon, or flying the kite, like you were searching for a key to unlock the Kingdom. Jim, it isn't right to fool with these things. It's . . . well, sort of like tampering with Providence."

"How does a man know until he tries?" He watched her, studied her carefully, for he valued her judgment, courted it now. He was a man full of uncertainties, and he wanted to turn in some direction but did not know which way.

"Wouldn't it be easier to move?" she asked.

"The good land's gone," he said. "And it takes money to buy what every man wants. A poor man can only have what other men do not want."

"Yes, that's true," she said. "But I still wonder why we do it. Why we get up at dawn and work until dark. There's never enough grass or enough water or enough of anything. I don't want it to break us, Jim, and it's not that I'm afraid of a few wrinkles, if I get something for them. And it hurts to see you accept it all without question, all the trouble and the long odds. You just fight and fight and get nowhere."

"Jennifer, a man don't cuss a piece of land because it's too hard to plow. He don't shake his fist at the sky because it never turns cloudy and rains. And when a man lays down and dies, it's because it's uncomfortable to die standing up."

"Fred Sales lays it on God's doorstep. I wonder if it helps him."

Martin shrugged. "He's got thirteen thousand acres. That's a lot of dust to be blowing in your face. I guess he's got to hold someone responsible." He looked at his son, who watched attentively. Martin reached out and tweaked his nose. "Grow up to be a man, son. A man who can stand up and not whine about every-thing. You'll have it tough, like all of us. So learn to live life, giving as much as you take."

"I want to be a city marshal like Cal McKitrich," Tad said. "He never has to work."

Jim Martin laughed and cuffed Tad lightly on the head. The waiter came with their dinner, and they ate, then went outside to sit in the evening shadows. The boy had gone on ahead, and he came along the walk with a stick, raking it against the porch pickets, setting up a steady racket.

"Don't do that now!" Martin said, and Tad stopped.

The boy cast the stick into the street and walked along, stomping on the loose planks, sending up a hollow clatter. He got too close to the edge and stepped on a board that quickly whipped up and knocked him asprawl. He sat in the dust for a moment, then got up and brushed himself off. Replacing the plank, he went on down the street.

"We could afford your staying at the hotel until I get back from Rock Springs," Martin continued. "Shouldn't take me more'n three days, round trip." He reached out and patted her hand. "You can take the boy to church."

"You're taking the wagon?"

"No," he said. "I'll try to borrow a horse from Fred. Some of his hands are in town." He shifted in the chair impatiently, and she knew how it was with him.

"Why don't you go now, Jim? You'll get back sooner. I'll tell Tad."

He was relieved, and he got up, trying to appear leisurely about it. A diner came out of the hotel and paused on the porch to pick his teeth, and Martin looked at him once before bending to kiss his wife. Then he stepped off the porch and cut across the street to the saloon to see Fred Sales about borrowing a horse.

# Chapter Two

Cal McKitrich stepped out of Herb Manners's place just as Jim Martin mounted the porch. The marshal put out his hand and touched Martin lightly on the chest.

"Care for a cigar before you go home?"

"I haven't time now," Martin said. "Thanks anyway."

He heard laughter, and his name mentioned, then a man slapped the bar hard and everyone laughed louder. McKitrich said: "You've had your drink, Jim. Stay out of there tonight."

"Is Fred Sales in there?"

McKitrich nodded.

"Then I've got business there," Martin said and pushed past him.

There was a crowd at the bar, gathering around Sales and Charlie Goddard, who had the dog before him, trying to make him drink whiskey from a glass. The dog whined and pawed the slick bar with his feet, trying to back up, but Goddard's grip was strong, and there was no escape.

Sales said: "Herb, it's the brand you sell."

"A dog can't drink out of a glass," one man said. "Pour it in a pan."

"Yeah," Goddard said. "Get me a pan, Herb." The bartender hesitated, and Goddard spoke more insistently. "Damn it, bring me a pan now!"

"Why don't you let him go?" Herb asked.

"You want to argue? Now get me a pie tin."

Martin observed this from just inside the door, and McKitrich had got up and now stood on the other side of the swinging doors, looking over them. When Martin

26

advanced into the room, McKitrich came in.

Sales and Goddard heard Martin's approach, and Goddard looked around. He was not completely drunk. It was too early for that, but he had enough in him to make him wobbly on his feet.

"Hey," he said. "You ever see a whiskey-drinking dog, Jim?"

"Yes," Martin said quickly. "Can I talk to you, Fred?" He took care not to look at the round, fear-set eyes of the dog, for the dog would stare at him hopefully, and Jim Martin did not want to be anyone's hope.

Goddard reached out and grabbed his sleeve, turning him back so that he faced him. "Where'd you see this dog? You tell me."

For a moment Martin was almost tempted, then he looked at the shivering animal. A dog didn't cry or plead, he knew, but it looked like he was trying to cry and plead. Casually, unhurriedly, Martin took Goddard's thumb and bent it back until he released the dog, then he tucked it securely under his arm and scratched his ears.

"My boy's been talking about wanting a dog," Martin said. "You didn't have any further use for this one, did you, Charlie?"

"Why . . . well, I was goin' to give it to my own kid, Pete." He reached for the dog, but Martin partially turned away, placing the dog out of Goddard's reach. This made Goddard angry. This, and the casual, untroubled way Martin had taken the dog. "God damn it, get your own dog!"

"I just did," Martin said softly.

There was a lot of trouble in this man, and perhaps he was looking for a way to get rid of it. This was a

27

common opinion of the men in the saloon, and they waited, silent, not moving, to see how this would turn out. Goddard stared for a minute then slipped his hand under his coat.

"One last time I'll tell you . . . give me back my dog."

"You don't have a gun under there," Jim Martin said. "You haven't worn a gun since the spring of 'Eighty-One when that Kansas man made you dance in the street. But I'll tell you what I'll do, Charlie. I'll let Herb hold the dog as stakes, then I'll fight you for him. If I kick the livin' hell out of you, Charlie, the dog is mine." He let a smile build on his face slowly. "The other way around, you can have him."

"You're crazy! I wouldn't fight over a damned dog!"

"Then I guess that's all there is to be said."

Martin turned to Fred Sales, and Goddard raised a hand to pull him around again but thought better of it. The time for correcting the mistake had passed, and everyone knew it and went back to their drinking and talk. McKitrich, who had remained alert and motionless by the door, came up to the bar and relaxed against it, turned slightly so that he could observe Charlie Goddard. The man had his head tipped forward, scowling, looking at the whiskey in his glass and cursing himself for not moving when he had the chance.

"I saw a few horses on the street carrying your brand, Fred," Martin said casually. "Could I talk you into my borrowing one?"

Sales thought about this. "You're still set on seeing that damned man in Rock Springs?" He took Martin by the arm and led him outside to the porch. "I know that old man, Jim. He's feeble in the head."

"So?"

"All right," Sales said. "Go to Rock Springs." He bent and looked at the dog that wagged his tail when Martin scratched his ears. Then Sales laughed. "God damn, I never thought you'd buffalo Goddard that way, Jim. What the hell got into you? Oh, sure, it was a joke. You bluffed him, and he went for it."

"Why do you think I was bluffing?" Martin asked.

Sales peered at him then grunted. "Yeah, I see that you weren't. Jim, maybe you ought to get good and drunk. Sometimes it helps."

Martin shook his head. "Will you loan me a horse, Fred?"

"Yeah, if you're that set on making a fool of yourself. Take Nolan's bay. He can ride home with me." Martin nodded his thanks and started to step away, but Sales took his arm. "Maybe this'll be a wet year. Why don't you hold off and see? There's time."

"You really think so? Good night, Fred."

He cut across the street, and his wife saw him approaching. She left the other ladies and walked away from the hotel so that they wouldn't be overheard by the others.

"The boy'll be pleased now," Martin said, handing her the dog.

She looked at the animal then said: "Isn't this the one Charlie Goddard called across the street earlier today?"

"I believe it is the same," he said. "However, Charlie had no more use for it. Sales let me have a horse."

"You're leaving now then?"

"Yes. Like you say, start early, get back early." He reached out and patted the dog on the head. "Better tell Tad to put a rope on him for a day or two until he understands where his home is."

29

"Jim," she said softly, tenderly, "you're a good and gentle man."

"Hmm," he said, then after a moment's hesitation he went down the street to get Nolan's horse.

She watched him go and, when she turned to go back to the hotel, Marshal McKitrich was almost to the walk. He had crossed the street with his customary quietness.

"Evenin', Missus Martin," he said, politely touching the brim of his hat. Then he smiled and rubbed the dog's muzzle. "The boy'll like him. I had a dog once. A big, hairy dog named Jiggs." He took a look up and down the street in the casual, attentive way he had then said: "Missus Martin, could I talk to you about Jim?"

"Is there something wrong?"

"Well, no. Nothin' that Jim's done. It's just this business of shootin' off the courthouse cannon and flyin' kites, and now chasin' to Rock Springs when he knows there's nothin' there." He rubbed a hand over his face. "Normally I wouldn't be saying anything, but I like Jim. I don't want him to go on being laughed at."

"What do you want him to do, Marshal? Sit on his porch and watch the land turn to dust?"

"Some things can't be helped," McKitrich said.

"Jim doesn't see it that way," Jennifer said softly. "He's got to fight, to do something, even if it isn't any good. That's the way he is. I don't believe he can make rain, but he's convinced he can, and I wouldn't rob him of that belief, because it must be a comfort to him."

"Someday he'll have to face the truth," McKitrich said. "It won't be easy."

"That's right. It'll probably kill him, just like it's killed thousands who went on fighting, not giving up. I don't find anything gentle and comforting in land, Mister

McKitrich. A man died for every acre in the country. It takes a man and uses his strength, and then it breaks him and swallows him, turns him to dust. But only the men who have to beat the land. Men like Jim. The weak survive because they quit before they're hurt." She sighed and shook her head. "Leave Jim alone, Mister McKitrich. Don't you see that you can't do anything else?"

"I guess you're right," he said softly. "A pity. He's a good man. Better than the others. But then it takes someone better to make the good fight." He puffed on his cigar and discovered that it had gone out. He threw it away. "Sales has never really had it tough. He's got the creek running through his place. And Charlie Goddard has that sink that fills with water every winter. And I guess all of the others have something to give them hope. But Jim's just got a bone-dry, flat piece of land. He's a smart man. How come he bought it in the first place?"

"Because he only had fourteen hundred dollars," Jennifer said.

"Yeah, that can force a man to take the rag end," McKitrich said softly. "Ah . . . when Jim comes back, I wish you'd have a talk with him, though. He crowded Charlie Goddard pretty hard tonight. Try to convince him that he has enough trouble without asking for more."

"What was it about? The dog?" She smiled. "I might have known it. All right, I'll talk to him."

"It's been nice chatting with you," McKitrich said, then tipped his hat before moving on down the street.

At dawn two of his hands carried a singing Fred Sales out of Herb Manners's place, put him in the buggy, then

31

drove him home. His disgusted wife remained in town, so she could attend church and present an unassailable front to the townspeople.

Charlie Goddard did not go home at all, which was not unusual, for Herb always put him in the alley before he closed up, and Charlie spent the night there, mumbling about the things he ought to have said when Jim Martin backed him up so neatly. His wife went home with the boy, for unlike Edith Sales she needed time to prepare herself for the next Saturday when she would have to go through this all over again.

Tad Martin got up as soon as it was light and went out into the alley behind the hotel to play with the dog. The sounds of their romping woke Jennifer, and she lay in bed and listened. Then she got up, washed her face, and dressed.

The dog liked to chase a stick and bring it back, and Tad sat on the back steps, tossing the stick down the narrow alley. Cal McKitrich found him there on his way to bed. He stopped and watched for a moment.

"What are you going to name him?" McKitrich asked.

"Gee, I don't know."

"He ought to have a name," McKitrich said. "Give it some thought, though. A name is important to a dog. And he looks like a good one." Heels clicked on the back stairs, then the door opened, and Jennifer Martin stepped out.

"Good morning, Marshal. Tad, tie the dog up and come in and wash for breakfast."

"Aw, I took a bath last night."

"Never mind. You wash now." The boy knew better than to argue, so he put the rope around the dog's neck and tied him to an old hitching post. To McKitrich,

32

Jennifer said: "Your day's just ending, isn't it, Marshal?"

"And it's always a long one."

"Why is it that lawmen look for more trouble at night than in the day?"

McKitrich thought about this and said: "I think a man wants the night to hide his darkest sins. The two go together." He went past her then and up the stairs to his room.

With the dog tied, Tad followed his mother into the hotel.

# Chapter Three

Jim Martin was still on the Rock Springs Road, nearer the mountains now. He figured to make the town shortly before noon, if he didn't stop to rest. He studied the mountains in the bland dawn light. They seemed totally different than when viewed from Morgan Tanks. The distance softened their harsh face and rounded the ragged sharpness of their shoulders. From Morgan Tanks they seemed inviting when they were not really inviting at all. But then he supposed it was always best to look at a thing from a distance rather than close up. A man never saw the flaws in anything until he examined it critically.

There was no breeze at all. The dawn was unearthly still, as though resting, gathering its strength so it could make heat and build a searing wind and make miserable the people who were presumptuous enough to gouge out an existence on the barren face of the land.

Martin dismounted and walked along, scuffing the dirt with his toe to find pebbles and, when he had a handful, he threw them to each side of the road, into the grass, trying to stir some animal or bird to life. He wasted his time and the pebbles.

At one time a railroad had run through Rock Springs. The tracks remained, but now it was only a spur line, rarely used except when the railroad wanted to park a few rotting cattle cars. Now and then a train came through, in the spring and fall, if there were cattle to be shipped. A yellow and weathered depot remained, and one man operated the telegraph and freight, but his duties were light, and he spent most of his time sitting on the platform, playing checkers with the town loafer. This was Jim Martin's destination, for he sought the man with the most time on his hands; that man, having little business of his own to mind, would know everyone else's. He would know where Patchin lived.

The two men saw him coming, and since traffic on the Morgan Tanks-Rock Springs Road was so light, a solitary traveler was an oddity. Martin dismounted stiffly and stepped to the welcome shade of the porch.

"Which one of you is the railroad man?"

"I am," the telegrapher said. He pointed to his sleeve protectors and celluloid visor. "Can't you tell?"

"Well, I'm looking for a man named Patchin," Martin said. "Does he live around here?"

"I be Patchin," the other man said.

He was a very old man. Martin suspected that he was eighty or better. Patchin's face was clean shaven, revealing a skin like wrinkled leather. There is about most men's faces something distinguishing, some outstanding feature, but with Patchin there was nothing a man remembered except that he was very old. The eyes were blue, or gray; they were so heavily lidded, it was difficult to tell. Yet they were bright, alert, very clear, like finely ground glass. Patchin's clothes were rags. He wore a faded green shirt with the sleeves cut off above the elbows, and the tail of it was tucked inside his underwear so that some of the waist was revealed above the line of his trousers.

"I be Patchin," he said again. "What you want, young fella?"

"Mister Patchin, maybe you can help me," Martin said.

"Nobody helps me. Why should I help you?"

"He's a little weak in the head," the telegrapher said. He took his finger and made a circular motion near his temple, a motion Patchin either did not see or pretended not to see.

"I hear you can make rain," Martin said, and the telegrapher laughed.

"Sometimes I can," Patchin said. "I got water on my place." He grinned, exposing pink gums.

"He dug a damned well and got water," the telegrapher said wearily. "Fella, you heard wrong."

"You've got an annoying habit," Martin said, "of talking when no one's asked you anything. Now, I hope I don't have to mention this again, because I've gone all night without sleep, and I'd just as soon boot you in the ass a few times before resting." He turned his attention to Patchin, who watched Martin unwaveringly.

"Did you try shootin'?" Patchin asked.

"Yes, and kite flying too."

"Fire?"

"Not yet. Should I?"

Patchin grinned. "Should you what?"

"Try fire."

Patchin looked at him for a moment then said: "I'm playin' checkers with this here fella. Got no time to talk now."

"You see how it is?" the telegrapher said. He shook his head, and Jim Martin understood how far he had come for nothing. He turned and led the horse on down the street to the stable.

Fred Sales had been right. This was just another of Charlie Goddard's notions of a joke. But then Martin had pretty well understood that before he made the ride, and still he felt there was an outside chance.

36

He grained the horse and leaned against a stall and rolled a smoke. From where he stood, he could see most of the street, and he decided it wasn't much better than Morgan Tanks. And not a lot better than the other towns he had been in. This was poor country. A man just couldn't get around that. Skimpy land with skimpy cattle trying to get enough to eat off a twenty-acre piece — that was about the ratio: one cow for every twenty acres of graze. If a man had a little water, he could hand feed and double his herd. Water made the difference.

His father had talked about making the trip west in '51. All the wagons had traveled across the vast sweeping prairie, and the only ones who stopped were buried there. It was Indian land, and buffalo land, and that was all. But a man had to have some place, so he took the bad in place of nothing. That was Jim Martin's fate, to come along when the good had been taken. He could not find words to curse a bad circumstance because he had never known anything better. He took it as a part of his lot and tried to stand up to it.

Later, he decided, he'd go on out to Patchin's place and look at the well, just to see what water looked like coming out of the ground. The trouble wasn't for nothing, he decided. Martin hadn't tried fire yet, and perhaps he could get the old man to talk about it some more.

Five hours' sleep in the stable loft made him feel better, then he washed at the pump before going down the street to a restaurant. Hunger was gnawing a hole in him, and he bought the fifty-cent special — a thick steak, two boiled potatoes, and a dish of stewed tomatoes. The steak was tough, and the potatoes badly cooked, and the tomatoes came out of a can, but it filled him, and he went back to the street feeling quite pleased with the world.

He watched the lamps come on in the town then gravitated toward the saloon and a glass of beer. There was a sprinkle of customers at the bar and three men at a table, playing cards. Everyone looked at him for a moment then ignored him.

"Beer," he said when the bartender came up. The dime and the beer changed hands, then Martin turned and put his back to the bar and looked about the room. An enormous pair of elk antlers hung on the opposite wall. Years before someone had hung a buffalo coat there, and it had never been taken down. The moths had eaten away most of the hair, and dust lay heavy on it.

A man down the bar turned his head and spoke to Martin. "From Morgan Tanks, ain't you?" Martin nodded. "I've been thinking of movin' there. Got a place in the hills now, but it's hell, runnin' cattle in the hills. You got it lucky on the flats, mister."

"I'm glad to hear that," Martin said.

He finished his beer and had his stein refilled. The bartender kept glancing at the wall clock. Finally he said: "It's a quarter after seven. About time for old man Patchin to show up, ain't it?"

"He's never been late," one man said. "What you got fixed up for him tonight?"

The bartender grinned and held up a bottle. "Linament. I put in a double shot. Gives it body." He set the bottle on the bar. "Now everybody keep a straight face." He looked directly at Jim Martin. "This is a little joke among us folks in Rock Springs, mister."

"What is the man, the town joke?"

"It ain't important what he is," the bartender said.

38

"You just laugh when we laugh, huh?"

"If I see anything funny," Martin said.

"It's goin' to be funny," one man said. "It always is, ain't it, Sam."

"Real funny," Sam said.

They waited for Patchin, and they didn't have long. He pushed through the door and stood there in his cast-off rags, giving each man his toothless grin. Then he approached the bar. He stood next to Martin but did not seem to recognize him at all.

"'Evenin'," Patchin said.

They murmured and nodded and waited. The old man looked at the glasses before everyone and licked his lips. The bartender said: "Got a little thirst, Patchin?"

"It's been a hot day."

"Well, you're in luck. The boss forgot to lock up his private bottle. How's that for sweet potatoes?"

"That's somethin'," Patchin admitted.

The next thing, Martin thought, they'd have the old man begging for a drink. That was all a part of it, to take away his pride, make him act shamefully, reduce him to a panhandler, then feed him doctored booze. The joke wouldn't be so funny if he didn't beg. Someday, Martin supposed, he would be like this, old and all used up and half gone in the head, spending his time cadging drinks and trying to remember just one thing pleasant from a distant youth.

"Maybe he'd like a beer," Martin said. "I'll buy."

"And maybe you'd better keep your money in your pocket," one man said softly. "That, and your mouth shut."

The bartender uncorked the bottle and poured a drink for Patchin. He was raising it to his lips when

Martin reached out and halted the motion.

"A man shouldn't drink alone," he said softly. "The bottle's open, so why don't these other gents join you?"

"What the hell you trying to pull?" the bartender asked. "This is a private invitation."

"I just thought I'd change it," Jim Martin said. He looked at the old man, who shook his head.

"Mister, you don't have to start a fight." He tried to smile, but there wasn't anything to smile about, so he let it fade to dull resignation. "They're goin' to have their joke, mister. I know it. They know I know it. I guess they've put nearly everythin' under the sun in that bottle, but I drink it anyway. That's the way the world is, mister. Your bed's been made, and you got to lay in it."

"Tonight you ought to sleep in the hotel," Martin said. He looked at the bartender. "Get him a decent drink or pull in your horns."

"We ought to take you apart," one man said.

"That ain't a bad idea," the bartender said and began to take off his apron.

Jim Martin smiled and flung himself over the bar. He hit the bartender flush on the side of the jaw, driving him into the back mirror and the shelves of glasses and bottles. Then he flung around and gripped the edge of the bar and kicked the man next to him flush in the face. The man skidded backward half way across the room and into some empty poker tables. That was the last blow Jim Martin landed.

They dragged him off the bar and smothered him, trying to get at him all at once. He went down, and they piled on him until he was no longer visible. They were like ants, all getting into the hill at the same time, and none of them making it. Because there were so many, Martin suffered less physical damage, although the weight of them drove the air from his lungs and made his head swim dizzily.

Patchin laughed and danced, then he walked around the bar and stepped among the shattered glass to pick up the sawed-off shotgun. He fired into the ceiling and, before the boom died, the men were off Jim Martin and standing there, staring at him, wondering how dangerous he was with a gun in his hands.

Pointing the shotgun at two of the men, Patchin said: "Take him outside."

They obeyed, and Martin groaned as he was carried through the door. At Patchin's direction, he was dumped in the horse trough, and Martin sat up, shaking water from his hair.

"Get back inside," Patchin said, "and don't stick your nose out." The two men seemed glad to obey and, when they were alone, Patchin put the shotgun down and helped Martin from the trough. "You hurt any, mister?"

"I feel damned good," Martin said. "Old man, don't you remember me at all?"

"Never seen you before."

Martin paused then said: "The hell you don't." His tobacco was a soggy ruin so he threw it away. "Old man, you ain't as gone in the head as you let on."

"You come with me," Patchin said.

"Where?"

"My place. Got somethin' to show you."

They stopped at the stable, so Martin could pick up his horse, then he walked home with the old man. He lived a mile out of town, near the foothills, and the house was a fallen-down mud shack with a solitary tree growing in the front yard. When Martin saw the tree, he stopped and thought how fine it would be to have that in front of his place. It would give cool shade in the hottest part of the day, and the boy could hang a swing in it, and perhaps he could build a seat under it, so Jennifer could sit there and sew. But most important, the tree would become a landmark on the vast prairie, and people would know of it from Dakota to Texas and look for it when they crossed the naked plains. However, it took water to grow a tree.

Patchin said: "Like my tree, huh, mister?"

"It's a good tree," Martin said. "Healthy, with sturdy limbs." He walked over and took a limb in his hands and shook it once. "Did this grow here?"

"Yep. Just a little shoot when I bought it. Some fella passin' through. He got it in San Francisco from a fella in Australia. Never seen anythin' like it, so I bought it and planted it."

Martin walked around the tree and stopped near a tin pipe. The pipe ran to the well where a storage tank held water, but the outlet of the pipe was at the base of the tree, and a trickle of water ran from it constantly.

"Shootin' and kite flyin' and burnin' is no good to make rain," the old man said. "To get water, you've got to plant a tree."

"How's that?" Martin asked. He wanted to hear the old man talk. There was something about him, a blend of madness and wisdom that made what he had to say important.

"Them rainmakers is all wrong," Patchin said. "Stop tryin' to get water to come down, mister. Make it come *up* from the ground. Now this is a special kind of tree, mister. You take a shoot of this tree and plant it and

42

water it faithful, and God sees it and knows you want water, so He puts water in the ground. I planted a tree first, that I did. Got water too." He squinted at Martin. "How bad you want water, mister?"

"Bad."

"Mister, you don't understand. Plant one of these trees, and you've got to keep it watered. With blood if you have to, but it can't be allowed to die."

"I'd plant my soul in the ground to get water," Jim Martin said. "Patchin, is there water out there on the flats?"

"Could be, but it won't come easy. The tree's got to be planted first, mister, and kept alive."

"I understand that. Will you give me a shoot from this tree? Not too big. I've got to take it to Morgan Tanks. But I'll make it grow."

The old man cackled and slapped his leg. "By God, you say that like you mean it! I said this was a special tree, didn't I? Here, look on the ground. See them shoots coming up? There's a big one, all one man can handle. But it'll have a thirst, mister. This tree's got a powerful thirst."

Martin was suddenly gripped in the excitement, the strangeness of this meeting, two men standing in the darkness, talking about dark things, talking about a tree that could bring water from the earth.

"How much you want for the shoot?"

"Ah, ah, don't rush it now," Patchin said. "Mister, you've got to understand once and for all about the tree. Make it grow strong and you'll grow strong in return. Neglect it, let your greed make you forget the tree, and you'll end up with a mouthful of dust."

"Jesus Christ, I wouldn't plant it to let it die!" Martin

43

shouted. "Will you sell me that small tree, Patchin?"

"Can't," the old man said. "Wouldn't be right for me to sell it. However, I don't have much. What you willing to pay for it?"

Martin knew a moment of genuine panic, for if the tree would bring water, its value was gigantic. Still, he didn't fully believe, and he didn't want to make a fool of himself or be a bigger fool than he already was. In his pocket was a twenty-dollar gold piece and some loose change. He said: "Patchin, I can't give you anything."

"It's all right," the old man said. "It ain't a thing a man sells. A curse, or a gift, is always given not sold. But on the way home you've got to keep it wet, mister. Them roots dry out one little bit, and she'll die on you."

"I'll keep it alive," Martin said, and he made it sound like a solemn oath. When the old man went into the shack for a shovel, Martin told himself that this was the most foolish thing he had ever done, to believe that a tree could bring him water. It was even crazier than firing the courthouse cannon or flying the kite. Yet he could not shake the possibility from his mind that Patchin was right. Nor could he shake the notion that he had to keep on doing something, even when no one else believed. He could recall his mother reading about the fishes and the loaves of bread, and the notion of the tree giving life didn't seem so far fetched at all. This wouldn't be the first time, he decided, that a fool had come upon a great truth.

He could not decide how Jennifer would take this. Tolerantly, he supposed, like the cannon shooting and the flying of kites. She seemed to understand that he was unlike other men. He could not stand by and wait

44

without doing something, exhausting every avenue of possibility.

Well, he'd take the tree back and plant it and water it, even if he had to steal the water from under Fred Sales's nose in the dead of night or go without water himself. Win or lose, Jim Martin would not hold back, and if the land got him, as it had others, then it would get all of him, everything he could give.

# Chapter Four

The church bell was ringing first call when Jennifer Martin put the finishing brush strokes to Tad's hair. He wore a new pair of overalls and a new shirt. The cloth was stiff with sizing, and the cuffs were turned up on the pants and shirt, just a little something for him to grow into.

"There," she said, "you look nice, Tad,"

The boy's face was ruddy from scrubbing, and his unruly hair clung wetly to his scalp. He brushed his hands against the legs of his new overalls. "I sure been doin' a lot of washin'," he said. "Pa washed me in the trough when we got to town, and I had to wash for supper and take a bath before I went to bed, and now I got washed for church. Sure glad I don't live in town. I wouldn't have any skin left."

"I'd like to have enough water on the place to wash when I pleased," Jennifer said. She smiled wistfully. "My, what wouldn't I give to have a clothesline with dripping clothes hanging from it once a week. That seems like a little thing to ask, but it's a lot to me." She sighed and put the dreaming aside.

"Can I take my dog, huh?" He saw her hesitate and pressed this small advantage, for he had learned that if she was going to say no, she would have done so without thinking it over. "I'll put a rope on him and tie him outside, and if he howls, I'll go right out to him."

"Well, I guess it's all right," she said. "But come along. That was first bell, and we don't want to be late."

She put on her hat and gloves while Tad ran outside

46

to put the dog on the rope leash. Jennifer stood in front of the small mirror and fussed with her dress, wishing that she had some material for ruffles or that she had taken the trim off, anything to disguise its age. In the general store she had seen some material that caught her heart and gave it a squeeze. She knew she could make a beautiful dress of it, but it was sixty-five cents a yard, much more than she could afford. And she hated to ask Jim for permission to spend the money. This last year had been so dry, and they hadn't shipped many cattle. She knew he was counting pennies all the time and trying to stretch what they had until next spring, after the rains, after the grass came up, and the cattle put on a few pounds.

Tad was waiting outside, and they walked down the street together. She erected her parasol and held it between them to afford shade. The dog followed them on a length of old clothesline. He was beginning to understand where he belonged now, and in a day or so the rope could come off forever.

The town seemed deserted, save for a few horses tied in front of Herb Manners's Saloon. A wind husked dust down the street and stirred the grass that grew from the cracks in the sidewalk. Flies gathered in buzzing droves around the manure piles littering the street.

They came to the corner and crossed over and, when they came to the alley, Charlie Goddard wandered into view. His clothes were dusty from his alley bed, and his face was puffed, the eyes swollen from whiskey and a poor sleep.

"Hey!" Goddard said. "Ain't that my dog you got there, kid?"

"My pa gave me the dog," Tad said.

His mother took his arm and said: "Come along. We'll be late."

"Hold up a minute," Goddard said and stepped clear of the alley. Farther down, and behind Goddard, Herb Manners stepped out on the back porch to discard some empty boxes. He saw Goddard and whistled for someone inside. Then he came down the alley, followed immediately by two other men.

Goddard heard them and turned. Manners said: "Why don't you come back with us and have a drink, Charlie? You look like you need one."

"*Agghhh*, leave me alone," Goddard snapped. He bent forward and peered at Tad Martin. "Ain't you the boy my boy licked?"

"He never licked me!" Tad flared. "Not in a million years!"

"That's enough, Tad!" Jennifer said.

"Yeah, I'd know you for Martin's kid," Goddard said laughing. "You got the same stupid look in the eye. When you grow up, you'll be just like he is, fifty inches across the shoulders and a half inch between the eyes."

"I think you've said enough, Charlie Goddard!"

He turned his attention to Jennifer and with mock gallantry swept off his hat and bowed deeply. "*Ahhhh*. Forgot my manners, didn't I?" He grinned and swayed a little, then he looked again at the dog. "Was meanin' to give him to my boy. You know, I think of them things, too. I think of my little Pete, yes, ma'am. That's my dog!"

Herb Manners took Goddard by the arm. He was forceful about it. "You're drunk, Charlie, and your mouth is too big." He nodded to Jennifer. "Go on, Miz Martin. I'll take care of this."

She hesitated a moment then walked rapidly on while

Charlie Goddard cursed and raved about the "dog-stealin' " Martins. Herb hustled him down the alley and into the saloon. He poured whiskey into a glass and shoved it toward Goddard.

"Charlie, what the hell's got into you, getting drunk every week like this?" He shook his head sadly. "God damn it, other men stay sober. Or at least they don't get as drunk as you do." Manners waved his hand toward the other two men. "Now, Al and Skinny don't get loaded to the gills. Why can't you be like other men?"

*"Don't lecture me!"* Goddard shouted as loudly as he could then stood there in the deep silence. "Don't lecture me, Herb. My wife does that. Don't *you* do it."

The two men, Al and Skinny, finished their drinks and turned to the door. "I'll see you next Saturday," Al said and went out, Skinny following him.

Goddard turned his head to stare after them. "I'm goin' to fire both of 'em."

"What for?"

" 'Cause they don't worry," Goddard said. "That's why. 'Cause they just take their pay and do their work and don't worry. Hell, a man's got to worry, Herb. If he don't, he ain't pullin' his load." He let his head loll from side to side. "I'm sick, Herb. Sick of tryin' and gettin' nowhere. I got troubles, Herb. God damn, I got nothin' but trouble. Cattle skin and bones. My sink dried up to mud. What's there to fight for, huh? You put your life and sweat into something, and it grinds you into little pieces and swallows you whole. Nothin' here at all but the ground to be buried in. Just a big, lonesome grave."

He bounced a silver dollar on the bar and staggered out. After moments of uncertainty he remembered where he had tied his horse and went down the street after it.

He had difficulty mounting, which angered him, for he considered his head startlingly clear, yet his muscles wouldn't obey his mind. He could not remember how much he had had to drink the night before. A lot, he was sure of that, for he had hoisted one for one with Fred Sales, until Sales fell to the floor.

His wife would be angry with him. He didn't relish the thought of facing her. She'd scold and cry and threaten him and bring in the boy's name like she always did, and he'd be sorry and promise, but he wouldn't keep it; he never had, for he had long ago passed the point where he thought a promise was worth the effort.

In the saddle he started out of town and, as he passed the church, he heard the singing and stopped as though fascinated by the people who went there to pray and sing and go home with everything unchanged. He wished he could do that, and his wife wished it too, but Goddard had never been inside the church. He didn't believe he could find anything there, not anything he wanted.

Among the parked buggies and tied horses he saw the dog tied to the length of clothesline. He stared at the animal for a moment, then dismounted and carefully made his way over there. Untying him, he dragged him back to the street and mounted. The boy had tied the rope into a slip knot. He was afraid the dog would get away. Goddard gave the rope a jerk and made the dog cough. He laughed and hauled in until the dog was hanging, gagging, choking, his hind feet barely touching the ground. Dallying the loose end of the line, Charlie Goddard flailed the horse into a run up the street, the dog banging and thrashing, beating against the horse's legs.

Herb Manners heard the commotion and ran to the

front porch and, when he saw Goddard's mad dash up and down the street, saw the dog dangling from the rope, he said: "Dear Jesus," and turned back inside, sick to his stomach.

With a wild, headlong rush Charlie Goddard ran his horse into the church yard, past the tied horses and parked rigs, and with a long, looping swing, threw the dead dog into the open church door. Then he whooped like an Indian and raced out of town.

The organ stopped, the singing stopped, and the first sound in the utter silence was Tad Martin's shriek of mortal grief when he saw the dog. He ran down the aisle and threw himself on the floor and clutched the dog to him, and it took a deacon and his mother to pull the two apart.

Not a person there was a stranger to brutality. The land had taught them early to be hard if they meant to survive, but they were accustomed to a reasonable brutality, not a senseless kind. Going to the door, the minister looked out and saw Herb Manners running toward the church. The minister waited.

"Who did this monstrous deed? Did you see it, Mister Manners?"

Herb nodded. He looked inside the church at the sobbing boy, and a tear came to his eyes because of the waste of it all. He wiped his eyes on his soiled apron then took out a handkerchief and blew his nose. "Charlie Goddard did it," he said. This seemed to be all he was able to say. He wheeled and ran back to his saloon.

The preacher waited a moment before turning to the stunned congregation. "Will someone take the boy to the parsonage, please? Missus Martin, you'd better go with him and comfort him, if you can." He shook his head sadly. "The devil was in Brother Goddard today. Let us pray it out." He spread his long arms as if to gather them together in one united intent.

Jennifer Martin looked at him. She had her arms tightly around the boy and hid his face against the folds of her dress. "The devil? Was that what it was, Parson? No, nothing that godly. It was meanness. Just plain, no-reason meanness."

"We must be charitable, even when it hurts us," the preacher said softly. "Charlie Goddard has put a mark on his soul today, sister. Aye, drunk that he is and knowing it not, there will be a tomorrow, and he'll be sober and know the mark he's put there. Come, let us pray for him."

"Yes," Jennifer said. "You all pray for Charlie Goddard, because when Jim learns of this, he'll do something besides pray." She started to lead the boy away, but he rebelled.

"He's my dog! He's got to be buried!"

"They'll take care of that," she said, fighting back the tears. "Oh, my dear boy, what a thing to see. What a thing to have happen. And for nothing. Just for nothing."

Tad stood there, tears on his own cheeks, watching her cry, then he put his arms around her for he was a male child and his duty was to comfort the female. He felt this instinctively.

As they crossed the yard to the parsonage, the singing began again, then it stopped, and they could hear the minister praying for the lost soul of Charlie Goddard.

# Chapter Five

An important characteristic of a saloonkeeper is his ability to keep his nose out of other people's affairs, and Herb Manners had been in business a long time. He stood around inside his place, slapping flies with a towel, and feeling his fury build until he could not stand it.

Closing the front doors and locking them, Manners shut up his saloon for the first time in twenty-three years, and this simple act made him pause and consider what he contemplated. But having gone so far as to close, he left his mind unchanged and took off his apron.

Leaving by the back way, Manners walked to the stable, past the church and the singing and the praying, and hitched his roan to his buggy. With whip in hand, he gave the horse a little touch on the rump and drove out of town, taking the south road toward Charlie Goddard's place.

For an hour he drove, hunched over in the seat, grateful for the shade cast by the top. Then he came to a pair of tracks leading off in a southeasterly direction, and the shade vanished. Coming in from the side, the sunlight baked his arm and shoulder until finally he took off his coat and laid it on the seat beside him.

Manners was not a young man, and he was not a very determined man, and his business was looked down upon by half the town, yet he felt a strong compulsion to act against Charlie Goddard. Not for Jim Martin's sake. Not even for Martin's wife or the boy's. But to act for Herb Manners. To act so that Charlie Goddard would never again mistake how Manners felt, or where Goddard stood in Manners's estimation.

The ride was long and dusty and intolerably hot. Finally he could see Goddard's place in the distance, a sprawl of frame buildings and a corral that needed repair. There was no grass at all in the yard just dust, ankle deep, blowing away with the wind and being replaced with dust carried on the wind from somewhere else.

The two riders who had left the saloon earlier came from the barn and seemed surprised to see Manners get out of the buggy. Al came over and cuffed back his hat.

"What the hell you doing out here, Herb?"

"Where's Charlie?"

Al shrugged. "In the house, I guess. He came home, and Skinny put up his horse. I guess he's in the house. I heard his wife yellin' her lungs out at him."

"And the boy?"

"Over to the sink, playing in the mud." He frowned. "What the hell's up, Herb? You closed up for the day?"

Manners did not answer him. He moved toward the house, pausing at the buggy only long enough to take the whip out of the socket. As he stepped onto the porch, Mrs. Goddard opened the door and blocked his way. She was a tall, thin woman with prominent eyes and teeth a little too crowded together in her lower jaw; they made her lower lip stick out, giving her a half-angry expression.

"My husband's resting," she said. "I don't feel I should wake him."

"I'll do that," Manners said. He brushed past her and entered the house. It was like a bake oven, storing heat.

She took his arm. "You're actin' high handed. Al! Skinny!" There was an element of fright in her voice, and she studied Herb Manners while they ran across the yard.

"Yes'm?"

"Mister Manners is going to wake Charlie. I told him he was asleep," Mrs. Goddard said.

Al looked at Herb Manners. Neither of them was armed, and Manners never carried a gun, but they could take him in a fight, and he knew it.

"Herb, you're actin' funny. You better give us the gist of it now."

"In town," Manners said flatly, "Charlie Goddard hung a little dog belonging to Jim Martin's boy. I just want to tell Charlie how I feel about it."

The two hands looked at each other then at Bess Goddard. "I guess you ought to wake Charlie, ma'am."

The emotion was all in her eyes, the regret, the shame, but her facial expression did not change. "He's my husband," she said. "I got to take his side."

"I guess you won't be needin' us," Al said. He tapped Skinny on the arm, and they went back to the barn, leaving Manners standing just inside the door.

Bess Goddard looked at the tips of her shoes. "Why did he do it? It was that whiskey again, wasn't it? I've begged him to stop drinkin'. Never a day passes but what I say, 'Charlie, will you please not get drunk again this Saturday night?' But he pays me no mind. No mind at all. He never sees the shame of it. Poor Pete, he's got a cross to bear, his father drinkin' like he does." She looked at Herb Manners. "What do you mean to do?"

"Don't know," Manners admitted. "I really don't know. Take this whip to him, I guess. Or talk to him. I won't know until I start."

"I'd fight for him," Bess said. "He ain't much, but he's

the best I have. He's got a gun, a rifle in the closet. I'd have to shoot if you hurt Charlie."

He could not understand her, the disgust she held for Charlie Goddard, and the loyalty she presented to the world. "Missus Goddard, don't you understand what a senseless thing he's done?"

"I understand," she said. "But a lot of things are senseless, still we do 'em. It's senseless to go on living like poor trash, fighting for every dollar we get ahead. Twelve years Charlie's been on this land, and we don't have a hundred dollars a year to show for it in savings." She waved her hands in a futile gesture. "Go on and talk to him, if you want. You won't make him listen. I don't think he can hear any more."

He looked at her for a moment and thought it would be best just to get in the buggy and go back to Morgan Tanks, but Manners was a stubborn man, and he did not want to have made the drive for nothing. "Which way?" he asked.

"The bedroom's on the right," she said and went into the kitchen.

Manners did not knock on Goddard's door. He just turned the knob and gave it a shove and, when the knob banged into the wall, Goddard raised his head and in a fuzzy voice asked: "Whazzat? Whazzamatter?" Then he saw Herb Manners and scowled. "What the hell you mean, wakin' me? What you want? Get it and get out."

"Charlie, I come out to tell you never to come in my place again."

"Huh?" Goddard wiped his hand across his face. "Aw, Herb, I was drunk. I didn't mean to hurt the damned dog." He slapped his legs and groped for an explanation. "I meant to go home, honest. But then I saw the damned dog, and he reminded me how easy Jim Martin had taken him, and I just wanted to take him back. Don't you understand, Herb? I didn't want the dog. I just wanted to . . ."

"Why don't you shut up?" Manners snapped. He raised the whip. "I came out here to use this, Charlie. But I guess I won't, now." He pointed his finger like a gun. "You just stay out of my place, you hear?"

"Where'll I get a drink?"

"Go dry," Manners answered and walked out.

Bess Goddard was waiting in the hall, standing by the wall as though hiding, and on her face relief eased the pinched look she had worn before.

"Thank you," she said.

This angered him, but he pushed it back. She had enough to contend with without his adding to it.

"He isn't worth much," Manners said. "Somebody ought to shoot him." Then he stepped out into the drenching sunlight and got into the buggy. Skinny sidled up and put his foot on the front wheel. "Herb, you hear of anyone wanting a couple of men, let me know?" He ran his tongue in the corner of his mouth. "I've been fed up with this place for a long time, only I didn't know it."

"You ought to stay for her sake," Manners said, nodding slightly toward the house. "And the boy counts for something." He lifted the reins and drove out, feeling that he had failed to do what he should have done.

# Chapter Six

With tenderness Jim Martin wrapped the ball of damp earth in a burlap sack, tied it, then bound this with another sack. The roots of the small tree were undisturbed, and the burlap, if wet often, would keep the earth soft and moist and the tree alive until he crossed the forty-mile distance to his own place.

He would have to walk it, of course. The tree was nearly eight feet tall, and he tied it to the saddle, securely, so it would not be damaged in any way. Sales's horse objected to this burden and kicked up a fuss, and Martin had trouble calming him, making him understand that this was his load, and he would carry it.

Old man Patchin was in the cabin, asleep, and Martin wondered whether he ought to wake him or not. He decided to thank Patchin again but, when he woke the old man, he did not recognize Martin at all. He was again in a fanciful world of dreams, some real, some very unreal, but it did not matter; he could no longer tell one from the other.

Martin knew that he ought to wait until evening before starting so he could travel most of the miles in the cool of night, but he was driven by a great sense of haste now. The tree had to be put into the ground, watered, tended, then he would be ready to dig his well.

Filling his canteen from Patchin's well, he put this on the saddle, then added a canvas water bag holding two and a half gallons. Martin drank a long time, thinking that maybe this time he could store up a little water and go till late afternoon before he would have to quench his thirst.

He underestimated the power of the sun, for by ten o'clock his throat was dry, and his lips felt like they were covered with clay. He also underestimated the thirst of the roots, for it seemed that they required a lot of water. Every time he looked at the burlap wrapping — and he did this quite often — the cloth seemed dry and parched, and he would uncork the canteen and soak it anew, then go on.

Heat danced in shimmering waves, and the dun-colored land glared in his eyes as tormentingly as the sun. By spitting on his fingers and mixing a little dust into mud, Martin made dark spots on his cheekbones and in that way cut out some of the glare. He kept looking at the leaves on the tree, and they seemed unduly withered to him, and he worried about this for he wanted above all for the tree to live. In his mind he had already accepted the fact that as long as the tree lived, he would live. He had blindly accepted, without explanation, Patchin's pagan belief, for he had exhausted his physical powers and could not whip the land and was now ready to call on strange gods to help him. Like most simple, direct men, Martin's conviction that the tree would bring him water became more unshakable by the mile.

He reasoned so in his mind. Simple, really — he would put the tree into the soil and water it, and the roots would reach out and draw more water. How very simple it was. He was surprised that this hadn't occurred to him before. A man was a fool to try to draw water from the sky. The answer was to woo it from the ground. Just like priming a well, and everyone knew that you had to prime a well with a little water to get water in return.

Sort of a little sacrifice of water to the water gods. Everyone did it and thought nothing of it. That was why the tree would give him water.

Martin's eyes burned from lack of sleep, and he had lost track of time, of the day. It was not difficult to do so amid such a great vastness. One day seemed so much like another that a person gave up trying to figure out whether it was Monday or Thursday.

He did not go to Morgan Tanks but bypassed it and went on to his own place. Probably he should have stopped for his wife and son, but he was thinking of the tree and how dry the burlap was and how he had only a little water left. Darkness was not far off. He had been traveling since sunup, and he was leg weary, but rest was something that would have to wait until later, until the hole was dug big and deep and full of water, and the tree was in the ground.

His place was a vague, dark shape in the distance, and night blotted it completely from sight while he was yet three miles away. But he traveled the remaining distance by instinct, walking along in a nearly total, breathless silence.

There was no time to fuss with a lantern, and he had already made up his mind where he would plant the tree, on the south side of the house where the sunlight was strong, where it would grow and spread roots deep. He took his shovel and dug like a man possessed, and then he put in the water from his precious barrels, and the earth was a greedy throat that drank heavily. But finally he saturated the hole, filled even so great an appetite, then tenderly unwrapped the roots, not disturbing the earth around them.

With the tree in the ground, he braced it with wooden

stakes to protect it against any evil and unpredictable wind that might come along and uproot it during its tender days. He bound the slender trunk with rope, lashing it to the deeply driven stakes, and at last he was satisfied. At last he could rest.

He did not sleep well or even very long and, when he woke, there was a soft, warm wind blowing, rustling the dried grass in the yard, softly whispering through the thick leaves of the tree. Martin did not relish the long ride to town and back, but it was something he had to do, so he saddled the horse and mounted up. He rode slowly, loose-bodied in the saddle, letting the horse pick his own way for this was one of those deep indigo prairie nights, starless, moonless. He could see no more than five yards ahead of him.

Martin could only judge the distance traveled by elapsed time. He thought he had gone four miles, then he stopped and raised himself in the stirrups, peering ahead. There was someone waiting by the road. Easing forward, Martin could make out the vague, dark shape of horse and rider. He said: "Hello there!"

The rider jerked his head around, cautiously approached Martin as though he expected trouble, and they met, stirrup to stirrup for an instant, but headed in opposite directions. Jim Martin reached out and took the bridle of the other horse.

"Is that you, Charlie? It's me, Jim Martin."

Goddard jerked back. He tried to rear the horse, to jerk the reins free from Martin's hand. But Martin held on with a stubborn man's determination to know what was going on.

"Charlie, what you doin', waitin' here at this time of night?"

Unable to jerk away, Goddard jumped off the horse and began to run, and Martin turned his horse and started after him. A new strength came to Goddard's legs, and he ran and jumped like a young elk, and Martin stopped and sat his horse, wondering which of them had gone mad.

*"Charlie, come back!"*

He yelled this as loudly as he could, and his words were absorbed by the land's immensity. Goddard did not come back, and Martin sat there a moment, trying to understand what new insanity possessed his neighbor. He hoped Goddard would stop running and catch the horse which would probably head for the barn.

Farther along the road came the rattle of a wagon, and Martin rode to meet it, pulling up sharply as he neared it. His wife halted the team.

"Jim, is that you?"

He dismounted, tied his horse on behind, then climbed up on the seat and took the reins from her. "Jennifer, I thought you were going to stay in town?" The fact that she was on her way home and the tone of her voice, when she spoke, gave him a new and sudden alarm. "What's wrong? Nothing's happened to the boy?"

"He's in the back, asleep," she said. Then she put her head against his shoulder. "Let's go home, Jim. We can talk on the way." She talked, and he listened, and she could not tell how angry he was for he did not show emotion as some men did, with cursing and threats or a headlong rush to seek revenge. She tried not to cry or inject her feelings into the telling. "It was a horrible, inhuman thing for Charlie Goddard to do, Jim. But he's sober now, and he knows what will happen."

"I just met him on the road," Martin said. "He was

waiting for somebody. You, I guess. But when he recognized me, he jumped off his horse and ran."

"Because he knew what to expect from you," Jennifer said. "Jim, I'm glad he's afraid. I want him to be afraid. I want him to jump when a door creaks or a timber in the house snaps."

He turned his head and peered at her, trying to see her exact expression. She was full of anger and hate, and had she been a man, he supposed, she'd take a gun and go after Charlie Goddard. "I don't want any man afraid of me," he said. "Why, I've never killed a man in my life! Sure, the boy's hurt. He has a right to be. But for me to hunt Charlie and . . ."

"Jim, I don't understand. And neither will anyone else in Morgan Tanks!"

This brought his anger to the surface, and he shouted at her. "*Do you think I care what they think? Does it really matter to me?*" He struck his fist against his chest. "A man is alone out here! He lives and dies alone and, when he dies, the people in Morgan Tanks will stand on the sidewalks with their hats in hand while the hearse goes by, and afterward they'll look down the road for the next man to come along and take his place. Damn it, don't you think I know? I stood there and watched Elliot ride by, and others, then bought their land at the sheriff's sale." He shook his head violently. "Charlie's been a bad boy, and he needs punishing all right. That's the way the town feels. Well, they can punish him."

"Jim, why did you give Tad the dog in the first place?"

"He wanted one, that's why."

"Jim, look at me. Did you take the dog from Charlie because you wanted him for Tad, or because you wanted to see if you could take him? How was it, Jim? If it was for the boy, you'll have to square this with Charlie. But if it wasn't for Tad, then it would be wrong to go after him."

"I've got other things to do," Martin said. "Don't you want to hear how I made out?"

"Yes. Yes, of course I do."

"I found this fella," Martin said, a new excitement rising in his voice. "What he said made sense to me, so I brought back a tree and planted it. Now I'm going to dig a well."

"Jim, there's no water in the ground." She tried to keep the impatience out of her voice, for she had seen him like this before, when he first started flying the kite and began shooting the cannon. He had a hope that needed continual renewing.

"You don't understand. This tree draws water." He laughed. "This time I'm going to hit it. I've got a feeling, a real strong feeling like I've never had before. Sure, I was excited about the kite and the gunpowder, but this is different, Jennifer. This feeling goes way down inside, and it's warm like a drink of good whiskey. I'm going to get water on that place, and when I do, I'll buy you a dozen pretty dresses and get Tad one of them thorough-bred dogs from Europe. I'm sick of livin' from hand to mouth. You don't know how sick I am of it, Jennifer. And all we need is water. Water to pump on a two-hundred-acre patch to make the grass grow. Why, my cattle would get so fat you could roll 'em to market. I could double my herd, or even triple it! Why, we could paint the place, build a new barn, eat store-bought air-tights, and . . . and have everything poor people don't have." He laughed at the thought of all this luxury. "God, I'd like to once walk into a store and know I could buy

64

anything in there without having to count the money in my pocket. And I'm going to do that one of these days, Jennifer. You just wait and see!"

# Chapter Seven

Without his horse Charlie Goddard decided not to walk home. Instead he went to the creek running along Fred Sales's property and bedded down for the remainder of the night. He slept a little and woke to a fresh dawn and a cloudless sky. Needing a horse, he thought that, since he was closer to Sales's place than his own, he'd go there and borrow one.

When he crossed the creek, he noticed how low the water was, and he paused to bathe his face and wet his shirt. Evaporation would cool him a little during the walk.

Sales's house and outbuildings were low on the horizon, and Goddard walked toward them. As he drew nearer, he could see that Fred Sales was home. The fringe-topped buggy was in the open barn, and the matched pair of bays was in the corral. In Goddard there had always been a shard of envy of Sales and the place he had built up. Of course, the creek made the difference, and Sales always ran twice as many cattle as another man whose water was scarce. As he approached the yard, one of Sales's riders left the barn and went to the house and, when Goddard came toward the porch, Sales stepped out the front door and stopped at the porch's edge.

There was no friendliness at all in Sales's expression. "What do you want here, Charlie?"

Goddard looked at him for a moment then said: "You too, Fred?" He was sweaty and dusty and tired, and his humor was foul.

"I heard what you did," Sales said flatly. "Jesus Christ, you acted like a damn' Indian! You ought to be locked up before you hurt somebody."

The door behind Sales opened, and his wife came out. She was a tall, slender woman with pale hair and wide-spaced eyes. Her face was oval and patient in expression, yet some deep yearning simmered behind the studied blandness. "Hello. Charlie, are you afoot?"

"My horse threw me, ma'am." Then he remembered his manners and took off his hat.

"Charlie and I were talking," Sales said pointedly.

She looked at him, and her expression did not change. "I could hear that. So I came out to see who it was. You don't attract many visitors, Fred." She put a hand to her hair and gave it a pat, then she smoothed her dress a bit, drawing the cloth tightly for a moment over a generous swell of breast. She was considerably younger than Sales, and she liked to point up this difference in subtle ways. Men attracted her, and she liked to preen for them and perhaps excite them. She watched Charlie Goddard's eyes and, when she knew he had seen what she wanted him to see and was thinking what she wanted him to think, she lost interest. Her conquest was complete. "I have some cold milk," she said. "Would you like some, Charlie?"

"Charlie has to be going," Sales said. "Can't you understand that, Edith?"

"It won't hurt him to drink a glass of milk," she said. "Come on in."

Sales scowled, and Goddard hesitated, then he stepped around Sales and went into the house. Sales listened to Goddard's step on the bare hall floor, and he turned to go inside also, then changed his mind and angrily stomped across the yard to the barn. The god-damned woman knew what irritated him the most, and she always made a great thing of it when he disapproved — this was his opinion and he wasn't about to change it. She seemed to take an almost savage delight in making him wait for her, inconveniencing him in public, doing things that were contrary to what he wanted. She had a hundred ways of making him feel small and unimportant, a hundred ways of showing everyone the contempt she felt for him even while she pretended to be a good wife.

From the kitchen window Edith Sales watched her husband walk across the yard, and by the stiffness of his back, the way he planted each foot, she measured his anger. Charlie Goddard sat at the table, a glass of milk before him. He loathed milk, never drank it, but felt that he ought to now.

"Fred didn't want me to come in," he said.

"This is as much my house as it is his," she said. Then she turned and looked at him. "Why don't you bring your wife over one of these days?"

"I . . . I'm going to be pretty busy for a while," he said.

Edith Sales studied him carefully. "Running from Jim Martin?" She arched an eyebrow. "Charlie, it's too bad you're such a miserable coward. Of course, you can always say that he started it, coming into Herb's place and taking the dog away from you."

"That's right," Charlie Goddard said. "That's just the way it happened. And the dog was mine. I picked him up, so he was mine."

"Then you ought to get Jim Martin before he gets you," Edith said softly.

She stopped talking when she heard her husband's

step cross the porch. He came into the kitchen and said: "Charlie, look out the window and see who's coming across the flats."

The happy way he said it filled Goddard with alarm. He peered out then swore softly. "It's Martin."

"It sure is," Sales said. "What you goin' to do, Charlie? Run or fight?"

"I don't want any trouble on your place," Goddard said. He turned to the back door, meaning to leave that way. "Fred, you ought to talk to him a few minutes. No tellin' what'll happen if he jumps me. I lose all control of myself when I'm riled."

"Bet you do," Sales said, enjoying this. "All right, Charlie, get going. But don't come around again."

He turned and walked to the front door, opening it as Jim Martin crossed from the barn. He had put up Sales's horse and, when he came to the porch, he said: "I put him in a stall, Fred. And I sure appreciate the loan of him."

"Find your man?" Sales asked it as though he believed Martin had traveled to Rock Springs for nothing.

"Yes," Martin said. "I've got some new ideas. Figure to bring rain with 'em, too."

Fred Sales chuckled. "Damn it, I've got to admit you're a hard-headed cuss when it comes to quittin'. Well, you know I don't believe in that hocus-pocus. But to be friendly, I'll drop over one of these days and have a look. What you got? Some new-fangled gadget?"

"No," Martin said. He seemed impatient to be on his way, "Well, I'll see you, Fred."

"Stay and talk," Sales invited. "Say, that was a terrible thing that Goddard did. You ought to take a gun and shoot him."

Martin twirled his hat in his hands and stood on one foot then the other. "Really, I've got to be goin', Fred."

"You going to walk back?"

"It's not far." He nodded to Sales, put on his hat, and walked out of the yard. Edith came out and stood beside her husband.

"Did he go?" Sales asked.

She nodded curtly. "God damn Charlie! He's a coward."

"So? You knew that. Edith, what's the matter with you? Why do you always want to humiliate me in front of people?"

"It's a way of getting even," she said.

"Even? In the name of God, what for?"

Her shoulders rose and fell. "For disappointing me, I guess. For letting me believe my life would be other than it is now, dirty and hot and monotonous."

"I never lied to you," he said. "Not one bit."

"Sure, but you left out a lot." She wiped her brow with her hand. "It's too hot to stand out here and jaw. I'm going to take a nap."

After she went into the house, Sales walked to the corral and cut out two saddle horses. Mounting one, he led the other and struck out across the flats in the direction of Jim Martin's place. He found Martin at the creek, sitting on the bank, soaking his feet in the water.

Dismounting, Sales took off his hat and wiped his forehead on his sleeve. "That water's mighty low, ain't it?" He nodded to one of the horses. "Can't have you walkin', Jim."

"I appreciate it," Martin said, "but I just returned one horse to you."

"Sure, sure, but keep him a while. He eats a lot of feed

anyway." He bent and cupped his hand into the water to drink. "God, I could stand rain. This creek should have a foot more water in it to be normal."

"A dry year," Jim Martin said. "Fred, was those God-dard's tracks I saw leadin' into your place?" Sales nodded. "Well, that wasn't the time and place anyway."

"I know. You ain't even packin' a gun."

Martin frowned. "Gun? Hell, I only wanted to talk to Charlie!"

"Huh? Charlie don't figure it that way. He knows what he's got comin'. Jim, you got a gun, ain't you?"

"A single-barrel shotgun. Fred, I don't need a gun. What you want me to do, kill Charlie for you?"

"Not for me. For yourself."

Martin was through talking. He mounted the horse Sales had brought along. But Sales wanted to talk. He said to Martin: "Jim, you've got to do what people expect of you or lose their respect."

"Hmm. I'll think about it."

"Everyone will be waiting for you to make your move. Don't disappoint folks now. This can affect you as much as what Charlie did. A body can get down on a man for what he does or fails to do about a thing."

This angered Martin, and he let it run into his voice. "Fred, I've worked my land hard as any man, and I've melted in the heat and taken no help from a soul. People have let me run my business up until now, and Charlie is my business, and I'll handle that my way without help. You tell that around."

He splashed across the creek then and rode toward his own place.

*"If I had anything against a man,"* Sales shouted, *"I'd take care of it!"* He waited, expecting Martin to stop or

answer, and when he did not, Sales got on his horse and rode home.

Martin put up the saddle horse as soon as he got back then walked from the barn to the house. The back door was open, and Tad was sitting on the porch, swishing a stick through the dust.

"I'm sorry about the dog," Martin said softly. "Tad, we'll get you another one."

"Don't want another."

Martin waited for the boy to look up, and when he didn't, Martin sighed and went on into the house. He stopped in the doorway, for Charlie Goddard's boy sat at the table. Jennifer was at the stove, peeling potatoes into a frying pan. Her glance touched Jim Martin, then she said: "Pete has something important to talk to you about."

"Why, sure," Jim said, hanging up his hat. "What's on your mind, Pete."

He was not yet twelve but tall and stringy for his age, and when he looked at Jim Martin, his Adam's apple bobbed with each swallow. Martin understood how much courage it took to bring the boy here, for the sins of the father washed off on the son. And Tad sitting on the porch wasn't helping any, with resentment, even hate, pouring out of him. Hate against Pete Goddard for something his father had done.

The boy wanted to be manly. He tried very hard, but he could not make it. Even as the words formed in his mind, tears came to his eyes. "Mister Martin, please don't kill my dad."

That a boy his age would even have to worry about such a thing shocked Jim Martin. "Why, son, what ever gave you the idea . . . ?"

72

"I heard the hands talking," he said. "I heard 'em say it would be a good thing if you took a gun and shot Pa!" He sniffled and wiped his nose on his sleeve. The tears ran down his cheeks. "Mister Martin, I guess he ain't any good, and he gets drunk all the time, but I got nobody else."

"Son, son. . . ." Martin reached out his hand, meaning to comfort the boy, but Pete Goddard jumped up from the table and edged toward the door. That he could read evil, danger in Martin's gesture, hurt him deeply, and he wanted to straighten this out, put it right once and for all. "Son, I wouldn't kill any man." He motioned toward the chair. "Come on and sit down. Jennifer, ain't we got some hoe cake or something for Pete to eat?"

"There's some corn bread."

The boy gave her no chance to get it. He wheeled and started through the door, then Tad came up off the porch like a released spring. He hit Pete Goddard in the mouth with his fist, then they howled and came together, kicking, biting, scratching, rolling off the porch and into the dusty yard.

Martin raced out, parted them with considerable effort, then took Tad by the arms and started to shake him. Pete Goddard seized the opportunity to run, and he dashed away like a frightened animal, positive that he was running for his life.

"His pa killed my dog!" Tad shouted, and Martin shook him again, very roughly.

"Young man, you've got a hiding coming," Martin said. "You've got to learn that when someone comes here to talk peace, you can't start a fight."

"Go on and lick me," Tad taunted. "Go on and beat

me, I don't care. I ain't goin' to bawl if you kill me. You see if that ain't so."

Jennifer came out, worry on her face. "Jim, please now."

"This has gone too far," he said. "The boy's got to learn."

He clamped an arm around Tad, nearly lifting him off the ground, and with the other hand he unfastened his belt and doubled it. He laid the leather on with some strength, whacking the boy's rump with a measured cadence, and then he grew tired of it and turned him loose.

Tad backed up and stared at his father through tear-filled eyes. He had not said one word or let out a cry, and the effort had cost him bloody lips. With both hands he massaged his smarting buttocks, then he said: "You ain't goin' to do nothin' to Charlie Goddard 'cause you're yellow."

"*Tad!*" Jennifer Martin's face wore a shocked, pained look. "Now you apologize this instant!"

"I won't!" he snapped. "I ain't never goin' to say I'm sorry, 'cause I ain't." He backed out of Jim Martin's reach and taunted him. "*Yellow . . . yellow . . . yellow . . . yellow!*" Then he turned and ran for the barn, crying openly now.

Jennifer put her hands to her mouth and stood that way, not weeping but ready to. Jim Martin's face was full of pain, then he whirled and smashed the leather belt against the porch railing. It whipped around, the buckle drawing blood on the back of his hand, but he did not seem to notice it at all.

"Jim, Jim, he's been hurt terrible," she said softly.

"Hurt?" He looked at her, his expression grave, dismal. "God, I wish it was the last hurt he'll ever know. Inside me, Jennifer, it's all scar from hurt. That's all that's there any more, just scars."

# Chapter Eight

Tad came to the house for supper, and he spoke civilly to his father, but he was taking nothing back, and Jim Martin did not ask him to. There was work to be done, work they could both do best together, so a truce sprang up, a neutrality observed politely by both sides, and this hurt Martin, but it was the best he could hope for.

After supper, he went out to look at the tree, and he was a little frightened by its appetite for water. The barrels were nearly empty, and the ground around the tree was not even damp from the last watering. Quite closely he examined the tree, the leaves, the trunk, and yet he could not tell what kind it was. He could not recall having seen a tree just like it. The trunk was thick and sturdy for a tree so young, and the leaves were thick and waxy, almost like skin to the touch. Martin had the notion that the tree would grow very rapidly if properly watered.

That was going to be the problem, keeping enough water on hand for the tree. Already he had noticed that, if he kept the ground around the tree very damp, the leaves stayed green and full. But if for an hour the ground dried out, the condition of the leaves changed, curling on the edges and showing wrinkles on their smooth surfaces. He accepted this as a visual warning and watered the tree from the barrels, using the last of the water.

Martin was impatient for nightfall so he could take the wagon to the creek and refill the barrels. That way, Sales or any of his men wouldn't see him. Sales was reluctant to spare two barrels a week. He would certainly object to Martin's taking more, but two barrels of water wouldn't last a week now. Two barrels a day would be more like it. He'd have to make the trip each night if he wanted to keep the tree alive.

Martin had already decided where he was going to dig his well. There was a slight mound elevation about fifty yards from the house, a bit of land just a few feet higher than all the rest. By sinking his well there, he would never need worry about the rains filling it with run-off water and silt.

Six to eight feet a day, he figured, a well ought to go that fast unless he hit rock. Then he'd have to blast until he got through it. And he'd have to case the well with timbers as he dug deeper to keep it from caving in on him. He wondered how big the tree would have to be before it drew water. Probably the smartest thing to do would be to start digging and in that way have the well ready when the tree started to bring water. Of course it was like old man Patchin said: *God saw the intent, and that was what counted.*

Tad came in around sundown. He smelled the flavors of cooking and didn't want to miss his supper. Martin said: "Harness the team, son. We'll leave as soon as it gets dark. I'll help you load the barrels."

Jennifer put the plates and silverware on the table, and they sat down. In the barn, one of the horses snorted, the sound loud and distinct in the silence. "Everything carries so far out here," she said. "Why, when we first moved here, I used to lie awake at night and listen to Shoemaker's dog barking three miles away. You remember him, Jim. He had that place to the east of us until the land killed him."

Martin laughed. "Jennifer, the land didn't kill him. He just got old and died."

"He was forty-six, Jim. That's not old." She put food on Tad's plate, and he frowned at the helping of vegetables she gave him. "Now you eat every bit of that," she said. "Jim, what kind of a tree is that?"

He shrugged.

"It seems a waste of water, planting a tree. Why, it ought to take a half a barrel a day just to keep it alive."

"Closer to two barrels," Martin said softly.

She frowned. "Well, you don't have to drown the roots, you know. Besides, most of the water just soaks into the ground before the roots get it. This ground is like a sponge. Two hours after a rain the ground's drying out." She reached across the table and touched his hand. "Jim, isn't it enough to have to break your back on the land to raise a few head of cattle without adding . . . this? Oh, I don't mean to complain or go against what you believe, but things need tending to, and you're just one man."

"I've got to let a few things go, Jennifer. The stock will drift a little but toward the creek, and if they cross, Sales's hands will cut them out and push them back. There was a time when a rancher here never saw his cattle except at roundup and shipping time. About all there was to do was ride around and look for wolves or rustlers. If it comes to a choice between losin' some cattle or getting water, I'd rather lose the cattle. With water on my place I can get more cattle. First things first."

They finished eating, and because there was still some light left, Martin passed the time by drying the supper dishes while the boy played outside. He lighted the lamp and went to the door a few times to look around. The shadows were growing rapidly deeper, darker.

"We can go in another twenty minutes," he said.

Tad came running into the house. He stood in the doorway, panting. "I seen someone out there," he said.

"Who? Comin' or goin'?"

"Sittin'," Tad said, an edge of fright in his voice. "It's Charlie Goddard, Pa."

"I'd better speak to the man," Martin said.

"I'll get your gun, Pa," Tad said and started for the bedroom.

"Hold on there. I don't need a shotgun to talk to a man who's been a neighbor for six years."

Jennifer stepped between them. "Jim, the boy wants a more understandable justice than talk. And so do I."

Martin frowned and looked from one to the other. "Tad's growing to be a man. He's got to learn that there's more to living than getting even."

"He's nine years old," Jennifer said. "A boy who's had something taken from him. Jim, if you put Charlie Goddard on the ground, bloody, senseless, he'll understand that. We all will."

His frown deepened. "It ain't right, everyone wanting me to fight him." Then he stepped outside and took a sweeping look at a horizon that was only a shade lighter than the black land. For a moment he could not make out a thing. Then his eyes became accustomed to the night, and he saw Goddard, sitting his horse, not more than a hundred yards from the house. Martin walked toward him, not trying to be silent about it, and he was within fifteen yards of the man before Goddard realized he was not alone.

With a whoop and a jab of spurs he wheeled his horse and drove it into a run, straight for Jim Martin. Martin remained rooted until he knew Goddard's intent, then he flung himself aside. Turf flew from the horse's hoofs, and Goddard yipped and shouted, drawing the horse up short, wheeling him for another run.

Martin knew that a man afoot was helpless, for a horse could outlast a man. Maybe a man could evade the animal for a dozen charges, but he would tire, slow down, and in the end he would be run down, trampled.

On the fourth charge, Martin miscalculated and the horse's shoulder grazed him, knocking him asprawl. Rolling, he was amazed at the power of the blow, and as he got to his feet, Goddard came around for another attack. Then a shotgun boomed and filled the flats with the sound, and Goddard broke off his charge. He sat the blowing horse for a moment, then dashed off, whooping and yelling to the night.

Martin stood there, panting, and his wife ran up. She held the empty shotgun and thrust it at him, half angrily. "Will you take it now? After this, will you believe you have to fight?"

"Seems like it," Martin said. He looked at the boy, then put his arm around his shoulders, turning him back toward the house. "Come on, son, let's go get the water."

Jennifer Martin could resent her husband's singleness of purpose, but she could not deny that he had the courage of his convictions. And the boy was softening now for he knew cattle and horses and men, and only a brave man could have stood up to Charlie Goddard out there on the prairie.

The boy brought the wagon to the house, and Martin loaded the empty barrels on the wagon. Tad wanted to drive the team, and Martin sat beside him. They rode along with the wagon clattering and the barrels knocking around in the back. Finally Tad said: "How come we got a tree, Pa?"

"Because land was meant to grow things, not merely for creatures to walk on. Funny, I should have known that, but it never occurred to me until recently." He mussed the boy's hair. "One day you'll have a stout limb to hang a swing on. This tree's going to be the most important thing in our lives, Tad. And we've got to care for it better than we care for ourselves. You understand?"

"I guess, Pa."

"We've got to keep it wet all the time, even if we have to put other things aside to do it." He put his hand on the boy's shoulder. "Remember, Tad, as long as the tree lives, we'll live, and we'll grow, and the land will be good to us."

This puzzled the boy. "You never talked like this before, Pa. Can things be different?"

"Yes, because we're going to dig a well and get water," Martin said. "You just wait and see."

At the creek they bucketed water into the barrels, and Martin was in a hurry. He did not want Sales or anyone to catch him dipping water at night. He was stealing, and he didn't like it.

Tad fell asleep on the way home and, when they got there, Martin carried him inside. Jennifer undressed him while Martin went out to water his tree. He came in later and washed from a shallow pan. She was wearing a nightgown and sat at the table, watching him towel his face dry.

"Are you going to start the well tomorrow, Jim?"

"Yes," he said. "There's no time to waste."

"No," she said, "I guess there isn't. Come to bed."

He wanted to stay awake and plan, but he was too

80

tired for that. Sleep hit him like a maul, and he woke with a start. It was almost daylight. Getting up, he started the fire so Jennifer could fix breakfast then went outside to lay out his tools.

Through breakfast he exhibited a great impatience and, when the first strong flush of sun drove across the prairie, Martin was outside with pick and shovel, digging. By noon he had a pit four foot square sunk in the ground, and Tad was kept busy with two buckets, hauling the dirt away. He had to spread it on the ground twenty yards away on the other side of the house.

Martin worked until nightfall, taking time only to eat something at midday and to water his tree. When he quit for the day, Martin had a hole so deep he could not quite see over the top of it. After supper he improvised a ladder from some spare lumber, figuring that, by the next night, he would need it to climb out.

The boy was in bed, and Martin and his wife were on the porch, enjoying a moment of silence when the sound of a buggy came across the flats. Jennifer said nothing, just went into the house for the shotgun, and by the time she came out with it, the minister had parked his slick-top rig and was getting down.

"Ah," he said, seeing the tree. "You've planted a tree."

Martin got the lantern and lit it, and the preacher walked around the tree, putting his face close to the leaves to smell them. "What a Godly thing, planting a tree." He clucked softly, then took the lantern from Martin. "Yes, it's a beautiful tree, Martin. Will it thrive?"

"If it gets water."

"Ahhhh, yes," the preacher said, as though reminded of something unpleasant. "It's a matter of water." He sighed heavily. "Such a graceless land, dry and hot and unpleasant. It's a pity a man chooses to live here. There have been times in my life when I've thought a man must want to punish himself badly to want to live here. Gold, land, and water . . . those are the things man thirsts for. They're all sinful desires, Martin. It's the devil in man that makes him want."

"I guess you came out here to make a point," Martin said.

"Ahhh, yes, I did. Charlie Goddard is possessed of the devil."

"So?"

"The town looks to you to take measures. Herb Manners had a burst of righteousness and refuses to serve him."

"Why tell me? Herb runs his own place. And he's old enough to know what he's doing." Then Martin smiled. "Or is it digging you that a saloonkeeper has more conscience than the church? What have you done to show Charlie Goddard how you feel?"

"I hold no conversation with the devil's disciples," he said and got into his buggy. "Martin, around here people like you. Don't do anything to change that."

He wheeled the horse and clattered out of the yard. Martin watched him go, then sighed heavily, as though another weight had been added to an already staggering load.

Jennifer took his arm and laid her head against it. "Jim, why won't they let you alone? If you don't want to fight Charlie, you have your reasons, and they're enough for me and for Tad, too. He'll understand."

"The town wants Charlie punished," Martin said. "Sure, he ought to be, but because I want him punished, not what the town wants." He slipped his arm around her. "Come on, we'll talk about it some other time."

After a week of digging Jim Martin knew that he would have to shore up the walls of the well. The dirt was already starting to crumble where the ropes came over the edge. He had to waste a whole day to build a windlass so the dirt could be raised, and he could be lowered and raised. And the tree had to be watered, a job that Jennifer and Tad shared. Every evening there was the trip for water. He rarely got to bed before ten-thirty or eleven.

There just didn't seem to be enough time in the day for Jim Martin, with the digging and the watering and fetching water. The night trips to the creek hid from Sales the fact that his water was being used at an alarming rate. And the tree still used more water than Martin liked to think about. He figured it was his imagination, but the tree seemed to have grown some, not in height, but in foliage, batches of pale green leaves.

He could dig no further without shoring, which meant a trip to town. Best that they all went, for Jennifer needed a few things, and Tad liked to play there. Watering the tree was a problem, and Martin was afraid to leave it all day. He pondered this problem a while and could find no ready solution.

Jennifer took it out of his hands by insisting on staying home with Tad. Martin knew that she wanted to go to town, for it was one of the few breaks from routine and boredom she had, yet expediency made him accept her suggestion, and he hitched the team and left the place. In the back of Martin's mind was the business with Charlie Goddard, and he resented the bother of it. A year ago he would have taken this up with Goddard immediately, fought him, and let it go at that, but he had more important things to do now, and he just couldn't summon the proper rage against Goddard.

The town couldn't know all this, so they waited for him to act and would condemn him when he did not. Martin considered this too bad, but it was all part of the price he would have to pay for his new dedication to getting water.

Hiram Daniels had some lumber stacked behind his blacksmith shop, and Martin made that his first call. Daniels was forming some harness hardware on his anvil when Martin came in. The blacksmith shop was a roof supported by four stout timbers so that any cooling breeze could enter and kill the heat generated by the forge.

"You still got those wagons out back? The ones you broke up for the wood and scrap iron?"

"I guess," Daniels said. "That's good oak. Nearly five hundred board feet."

"How much for the lot?"

Daniels considered it a moment then said: "Twenty-five dollars."

Martin frowned. "That's a lot for used oak, Hiram."

"Yeah, I guess it is," Daniels admitted. "But I don't much care whether I sell it or not."

This offended Martin at a time when he could not afford to be offended. Lumber was scarce, and all of it had to be shipped in from the mill three hundred miles away. "Well, I've got to have it," he said. "I'll go to the bank and draw out the money." He started out then turned back. "I guess you'll throw in the nails, huh?"

"Nails is ten cents a pound," Hiram Daniels said. He put down his hammer and tongs and came over to Jim

Martin. "I was in church when Goddard killed the dog. I've never been so mad in my life."

"Hmm," Martin said, his lips pursed. "I guess that has an effect on the price of lumber."

"A man ought to do something, Martin."

"All right, you're a man. You do it."

"He's not my boy. Oh, I heard about how busy you are, tryin' to make rain, but a man's got to take the time to settle accounts. Either that, or have people look down on him."

"I'll get your money," Martin said.

"Suit yourself, Martin, but I won't guarantee the wood'll be here when you get back. Quite a few been asking about it."

"Like hell," Martin said and walked down the street to the one-room bank. Kinred ran it himself. Business was too poor to employ a teller. The room was divided by a long counter and a wooden wicket cage. Max Kinred was always there, pen in hand, going over his accounts.

He looked up as Jim Martin entered. With aggravating slowness, Kinred put down his pen, after wiping it thoroughly, then closed his books. His glance lifted to the front window, and Martin turned his head for a look. Daniels was coming out of Herb Manners's place, and a dozen men followed him, all taking a place in front of the feed store.

"That's a good place to watch from," Kinred said.

"Watch what?"

Kinred smiled. "Jim, do you really think you're getting out of town without facing Charlie?"

They were minding his business, tending to his affairs, and Martin's anger began to rise. But he kicked it in place and said: "Mister Kinred, I ought to just walk out and see who'll stop me."

"Do that and you're through," Kinred said. "Jim, face it. The town's decided for you."

There were some things a man could not sidestep, and Martin recognized this as one of them. He stepped to the door and stood there, looking across the street at the men who waited.

Finally one of them asked: "Well, Jim?"

This was a simple question and demanded a simple answer. Martin gave it to them when he carefully took off his hat and laid it on the boardwalk. Then he took off his shirt and rolled the sleeves of his underwear. One of the men whooped and ran down the street, two others following him. A fringe crowd began to gather. Some stood in the doorways, and even the ladies came to the hotel porch or stepped out of the stores, for what Charlie Goddard had done offended them as much as it had their men.

The school bell started to ring, and by the time the three men came back, half dragging Charlie Goddard, the school children were gathered along the edge of the crowd. Martin looked at their faces, trying to find Pete Goddard, hoping all the while that he wouldn't be there.

Goddard was standing alone now in front of the crowded feed store. He had both fists clenched at his sides. Martin looked at the man and hardly knew him, for Goddard was unshaven and dirty and alone in his mind, which is a terrible way for any man to be.

"Why did you do it, Charlie?" Martin asked, and his words rang heavily in the silence of the street.

"He was a stray," Goddard said. "Somethin' I'd found." He spread his hands in an appeal for understanding.

86

"In all the years I've eaten dust and melted in the heat, I've never found nothin' that didn't put an ache in my back. But I found the dog, Jim. This damned little no-account dog. Found him and didn't know what to do with him afterward." He shook his head sadly. "I guess he was a good little dog."

"He was better than you!" Herb Manners snapped.

Goddard whirled and faced the men. "You sonsabitches! One of you step out here! Come on, you want a fight, then step out here! God-damned bunch of cannibals!"

"There's been enough talk," one man said. "Let's get this over with, Jim."

# Chapter Nine

*Whaappp!* That was the sound of Martin's fist striking Charlie Goddard in the mouth, and Goddard had stood there, waiting to be struck, as though he had to suffer the first blow. He was flung back, but recovered his balance quickly, and raised a hand to the blood on his smashed lips.

From the crowd there came a sighing, as though some inner tensions had been released, and they waited, all eyes fixed on Charlie Goddard. Martin felt their attention shift from himself to Goddard and wondered why, but he could not wonder long for Goddard was stung and wanted to get even. He tried to bullrush Martin, who stood solidly and knocked down Goddard's flailing arms and struck him again in the face.

There was very little science in either man's fighting. They hacked and mauled each other, with Goddard getting the worst of it, not because he fought less skillfully, but because he was supposed to get the worst of it. The crowd had decided long before the fight started who was going to get licked.

Both men were bleeding from cuts on the face. They struck and grunted, and stamped the ground, and kicked at each other when they could not land a blow with their fists. The onlookers were fascinated, stone silent, as though they were witnessing judgment and sentence all rolled into one.

Goddard's face was puffed and discolored, still he fought, his flailing arms going without exact direction. He considered himself fortunate if a blow landed. His only duty was to stand there and swing.

Neither man was knocked down, although they each staggered once or twice when a blow caught them squarely. Martin was breathing hard, tiring rapidly, and Goddard seemed hardly able to stand. He swung a kick at Martin, and missed, falling against him. Martin brought up his knee, catching Goddard squarely in the crotch.

Howling, gagging, Goddard fell back, half in the street, half on the board walk. His shoulders came down on the overhanging end of a board and it flew up, catching him solidly on the back of the head. He yelped again and grabbed it just as Martin came at him, meaning to finish this and be done with it. He swung as Martin kicked, and no one could say who connected first, although neither man missed. Goddard took the boot on the jaw and flopped back unconscious, and Martin grunted and danced in a short circle, the board clinging to the calf of his leg, held there by a nail driven into the flesh. He grabbed the board, pulled it free, and blood began to soak his pant leg.

Then he threw the board into the street and looked at the crowd. "He's been punished," Martin said between puffs for wind. "Now you can forgive him."

Herb Manners looked at Goddard. The man beside Manners said: "Give me a hand. We'll take him in the saloon."

"Not my saloon," Manners said flatly. Then he looked at Jim Martin. "You hurt any?"

"What does it matter?" He turned down the street, limping, and Manners followed him.

"Wait, Jim," he said.

Martin shot him an angry glance. "You got what you wanted."

"It was something you had to do," Manners insisted.

Jim Martin stopped then and faced him. "You damned fool! It's poor Charlie now. He's been punished and forgiven. God damn, I knew this would happen. I wanted him to walk around with his tail between his legs. Jesus, I did him a favor."

"Maybe, but we all won't let this go, Jim. Charlie's got to buy his booze some place else. I meant what I said."

He was sincere, Martin saw, and that took the edge off his resentment. He smiled and slapped Manners on the arm. "All right, Herb, we'll let it go."

"You've got a bad dig there on the leg," Manners said. "The doc will be back this evening. You ought to stay over and have him look at it."

"No time," Martin said.

Manners shrugged. "Jim, tell the boy about this. He'll be proud of you."

"If he was a man," Martin said, "he'd be ashamed."

He left Manners standing there and walked on to the blacksmith shop. The price of used oak, it seemed, had gone down pretty sharply. Martin bought it for three dollars, and the blacksmith threw in the nails for nothing and helped him load it. Then Martin drove out of town, holding the reins lightly for his hands were stiff and swollen, and the calf of his leg throbbed with each pump of his heart. When he got home, he'd have to put some turpentine on that or risk infection. And he didn't know what Jennifer would say about the marks on his face. She'd fuss and scold, but she wouldn't mean any of it. His hands worried him the most, for he had to work on his well and their being so swollen and sore would slow him down.

The boy would be glad he had fought. This would square everything and make him sorry he had said angry things. Martin was hurt by this for he didn't want the boy to be sorry for anything. Tad's desire for revenge was normal. All people wanted it when they had been hurt. But as a man got older, one of the earmarks of maturity was the putting aside of notions like that. The good with the bad, that was the way it came in life, and unless a man was lucky, a lot more bad came his way than good.

The tree had been faithfully watered. He saw that as soon as he drove into the yard. Tad was playing in the barn with a piece of rope tied to one of the beams, swinging back and forth, back and forth. He let go of the rope and ran to Martin as though he were terribly glad to see him.

Jennifer came out, saw the blood on Martin's pants, saw the discoloration and puffiness of his face. She said: "You fought him?"

"Yes."

"You whipped him, huh, Pa?"

Martin nodded. "He couldn't get off the ground." Then he looked at the boy, cupping Tad's face in his hand. "Do you feel better now?"

The boy was puzzled for a moment. "No. I thought I would, though."

"Then remember this as a lesson. You'll never feel better afterward for getting even." He gave Tad a slap on the rump. "Grain the team but leave them harnessed. We have to get water."

As he led the team and wagon away, Jennifer said:

"There's blood on your pants. And you're limping,"

"A man can't fight without getting hurt," Martin said.

He had to work slower than he thought, and even with the boy's help it was late afternoon the next day before the wood was unloaded. Then he began to erect the shoring in the well, starting at the bottom, with a lantern and hand tools. For two days and part of each night he worked, and it went slower instead of faster for his hands were broken. He felt sure of this. And his leg gave him an increasing amount of pain.

There was never enough time for any of them now. Jennifer and the boy hauled the water, and watered the tree, and helped him in and out of the well until he could no longer even do that. The wound was puffed and inflamed and sore to the touch, and he tried bathing it in hot water, but the swelling did not go down. Sleep was increasingly difficult, and he rolled about and dreamed about a hot wind coming in from the south and withering his tree. He woke in a sweat and sat up in bed, shivering and laboring for breath.

He got up without waking his wife, rolled a cigarette, then padded outside, and sat on the ground by the wall, feeling the night wind on his hot face. He was going to be sick. He had a certain feeling about it, and he began to make plans. Things would have to be taken care of and no mistakes made, and the responsibilities would have to be shared, each of them doing what they could. Returning to the bedroom, Martin shook his wife, and she woke immediately.

"What's the matter?"

"Come on outside," he said softly.

This was an unusual thing for him to ask. She quickly

put on a robe and went out with him. He pulled a chair around on the porch so that she faced him as he sat on the railing, favoring his leg. "Feel that wind? Worth getting up for, isn't it?"

"Jim, what's the matter?"

She was alarmed, and he didn't want her to be. "I'm going to be laid up a spell, Jennifer. Think you and Tad can manage? It's this leg. Givin' me hell, more every day. Likely I'll go out of my head, but you got to understand that, make allowances for it."

"Jim, we'll get the doctor!"

"No, I don't want you leavin' the place. It'd be too much for the boy alone, and someone's got to water the tree. Jennifer, Tad's got to water that tree and haul water every night. You understand? It's got to be done, no matter what."

"All right, Jim."

"God's made us all tough so we can live with these things," he said. "This infection's got to be taken care of. That's your job, Jennifer, tendin' me until I'm well again."

"Jim, I wouldn't let anything happen to you. I love you."

"Sure. Sure you do. You'll have to watch for the fever. I can feel it comin'. And later you might have to open the wound with a knife. Just jab it in and start cuttin', but tie me in bed first." He reached for her hands and cradled them against the roughness of his cheeks. "God, I wish I could give you more than this, Jennifer. I've been a trial to you from the beginning." She started to speak, but he held up his hand, cutting her off. "And the boy . . . I wanted it good for him. It's a pity he has to grow up in such a hard land. A boy should know more tenderness. Not from us, but from the earth. There ought to be coolness and gentleness and good things, and the boy has had none of this. Come on, help me into bed, old girl. And you do what's right, huh? Even when it hurts?"

# Chapter Ten

Martin's dawn was a grayness, full of pain, and he could not make the room stop swimming. The boy came over to his bed and looked at him with his large serious eyes, and Jennifer was always there, bathing his face and talking to him softly. He was more than sick. The vomiting went on, even when his stomach was pumped dry, and after each spell he had lucid moments when he would lay there, slick with sweat, and know truly how bad a shape he was in. And every time his wife would bathe his face, he would push her hands away and tell her to water the tree, water the tree.

He raved and was tied in the bed, and his dreams were long and fantastic, full of green lands and running water everywhere and a million trees like his own, only bigger, greener, shadier. And Jennifer was there, the woman he had carelessly loved and left was there, and the boy between them, and there wasn't much work at all, and all a man had to do when he was thirsty was to step a few paces to a spring and drink of water that was always cool and sweet.

Jennifer knew he needed a doctor, but there was no way she could go into town after him, not with so much to do. Martin required constant attendance, and the tree needed constant attention, and the boy was either hauling water or pouring water or hitching up to go get more water. She didn't think either of them would ever get to rest.

He needed a doctor to open the wound, to clean it properly, and she decided to send the boy rather than go herself. She told him what had to be done, and he took Sales's horse, striking out, and then she felt terribly alone. She knew the boy had been working hard, but she had no idea how hard until she tried to do his work in addition to her own. Each moment she was forced to leave Martin alone was a worry and a hand pushing her to greater haste, and in a fashion she managed, not by finding new strength, but by cutting corners a little, cheating on each job until it fitted the hours in a day. The tree was watered but not as much as it should have been, and the house stayed dirty, and the dishes piled up in the sink.

Then Tad came back with the doctor, and she went outside while he worked. Jennifer's head ached, and her arms ached, and she tried to remember when she had slept last, or the boy had slept. His eyes were dark-rimmed and sunken in his face. Martin cried out, and she jerked around, ready to go to him, then she remembered that he was being tended.

Finally the doctor came out, closing his bag. He had his hat in his hand and his coat over his arm. "He'll sleep now. I've drained the wound." He walked over to his buggy and tossed his bag on the seat. "In a few days he ought to know where he is, Missus Martin. Just see that he's covered and comfortable."

"Doctor, we'll pay you as soon as Jim's up and able to come to town."

"That's all right," he said. Then he looked from one to the other. "And get some sleep, both of you. You're both worn to a frazzle."

They watched him drive away, and then they turned to their work again. There seemed to be no end to it. For Jennifer there was the house to put in order. She had let everything go in order to tend her husband. Tad had the tree and the stock to take care of, and the trip to town had put him far behind. It was the way of the land, never letting up on anyone. You did what had to be done and kept on doing it and, if you missed a day, it had to be caught up somehow, no matter how tired you were. It accepted no excuses.

Martin's first clear consciousness came in the late afternoon, and he lay in bed, watching the slanted rays of the sun come through the open doorway. Turning his head, he saw the boy asleep on the floor by the stove. He was an unwashed, exhausted little boy who had gone as far and as fast as he could go, then stopped.

Jennifer was asleep in the chair, crumpled half over so that her head lay on the table, her arms dangling below it. Turning slowly, Martin tried to sit up, but he was so weak he could barely raise his shoulders. By rolling, he got to the floor, almost crying out when he bumped his leg against the bed rail. He remained there for a moment, resting, gathering his feeble strength. By gripping the bedpost, he pulled himself half erect, high enough to look at himself in the mirror hanging on the wall. He did not recognize himself at all. Many pounds lighter, his cheeks were bearded and hollow, and the framework bones of his face were hard ridges beneath the flesh. His lips were cracked and peeling, as though he had covered them with heavy wax and forgotten to take it off.

"Jennifer?" He turned and looked at his wife, but she did not move, save for the steady rise and fall of her breathing. Martin knew that trying to wake her would be useless. She was exhausted, and he would have to do for himself until she was rested.

By a slow, painful process of dragging himself, Martin got to the door. He rested there for a while then pulled himself into the yard. His first thought was for the tree, and he pulled himself to it and saw how curled the leaves were, how dry the ground was beneath it. Almost in panic he worked himself to the water barrels and pushed both of them over. They were empty. And from the condition of the wood, dry on the inside, he knew they had been empty all day and maybe the day before too.

It was hard for him to think of losing. Tears formed in his eyes. He crawled back to the porch, where there was shade, and sat there, his clenched fists on his thighs. "It's a big job I gave them to do," he said softly. The tears of defeat and frustration lay on his cheeks. "Just a woman and a boy, and a big job. But they're my hands now, my strength, and God, give 'em a rest if You must, but wake 'em before the tree dies." He let his chin rest on his chest. "I've failed my family, so it's a poor time for me to be callin' on You. I've been a sinner too long to expect a favor. But she's just a woman, and he's a small boy doin' a man's work. Neither has the strength they need, so help 'em if You can. Maybe You don't think I deserve water. I don't blame You if that's the way it is. But all men make their fight, good or bad. It's the way You made the world. We've tried to keep the tree alive. Tried and failed, for there's no strength in me to fetch water, and none in my wife and boy. Can't You see I tried? Can't You help a little now, just a little?"

He felt a little foolish for having prayed. He was like most sinners trying to reach God in one desperate try, afraid he had failed, afraid he would fail. For some time Jim Martin sat there, trying to make himself understand that this was the end, and he would have to accept it.

Try as he might to beat it, the land had finally broken him, and he wondered if he should curse or cheer because it was over.

The day was growing darker and, when he looked up, the sunlight was gone. Had he been sitting there that long? He didn't think so, unless his mind had wandered again. Yet the sky was growing rapidly darker, much darker, and he looked around to see what caused it. They were the blackest clouds he had ever seen, rolling and building all around him. They tumbled and rolled and grew thicker and darker and more menacing, then the wind began to pipe up from the northeast, a strong, cold wind with the smell of rain in it. He saw the first drops hit, like small liquid bombs, raising puffs of dust in the yard, then there was a torrential gush of water, a deluge of it, solid sheets that hammered the roof and pounded the yard into instant mud.

Martin had never seen a rain like this, not even a Texas cloudburst. Within minutes water gouged rivulets into his land, into his yard, and sought out every leak in the roof, dripping and soaking the wood floor.

Quietly Martin put his face in his hands and cried, for he had been heard, and he had been answered. When the emotion passed, he lay on the porch and watched the rain come down unbelievably heavy, a steady downpour. Runnels of water cut across his yard and bore through the small irregularities in the earth, and like spokes of a wheel converged on his well, filling it until water gushed over the top. He watched this and wondered how much water would stay in the well for the ground seemed to soak up the rain as fast as it fell.

When the rain stopped, it did so quickly, and the winds blew the clouds away, leaving a fresh and clean sun to wash over the land. There was a rainbow, and he studied the bright colors for a while, then it went away, and evening came with its darkly graying shadows. Martin fashioned a crutch, and went into the muddy yard, hobbling over to his well. It was full of water, full to the level of the land, while all around him, the water was soaking into the earth, leaving mud that would dry in tomorrow's heat.

God had answered him, he knew for certain now. God had watched him nurse the tree, watched the boy wear himself out tending it, and this was his reward, water at hand until he recovered from his illness. Martin stood straight now, feeling stronger than he had ever felt in his life, feeling cleaner, and he blessed the sense of desperation that had led him to old man Patchin.

The boy was awake when he returned to the house and, when Tad saw him, he ran to him and hugged him and cried. "Now, now, none of that," Martin said gently. "Did you hear the rain?"

"I slept, Pa."

"Go out and take a look," Martin said, then stood in the doorway while Tad ran barefoot in the muddy yard, stamping his feet, making mud squirt between his toes. Martin laughed, watching the boy, then went on in and shook his wife. She stirred, opened her eyes half way, then sat bolt upright.

"Jim!" Her arms went around him, and he held her, stroking her hair, letting her cry and laugh at the same time.

Finally he pushed her away slightly so he could look at her. "It rained, Jennifer. I prayed for rain, and it rained." He lifted her. "Come on, look."

Tad came in, tracking mud on the floor. "I'll bet the creek's bustin' its banks, Pa. Can I go over and see?"

"Sure," Martin said. "What day is this?"

"I don't know, Pa."

"It's no matter. Don't be long now."

The boy ran to the barn and got out one of the horses. He scorned a saddle, dashing away bareback. Jennifer went to the door and looked at the soggy yard. She saw the well brimming with water and turned to him, puzzled.

"Why doesn't it soak into the ground, Jim?"

"I don't know," he said. "I don't think it was supposed to." He pointed to the rain-gouged rivulets that marked the water's path to the well. "When I dug, I picked what I thought was high ground. Still the water ran to it."

She studied the land a moment, then said: "I think it's lower than the rest, Jim. It just looked higher."

"I'm goin' to shave," he said. "And use all the water I want."

She took a bucket, splashed to the well, then put it on the stove to heat. Martin moved the mirror from the wall to the kitchen table and stropped his razor. Jennifer watched him, then went for more water, heated it, and filled a large wooden tub.

"This isn't Saturday," she said, "but it's a luxury I can't pass up." Quickly she slipped out of her shoes and dress and petticoats, and stepped into the tub. He laughed and picked up his crutch, hobbling to the porch to sit in his favorite chair. Jennifer sang and splashed water, and Martin listened to the sounds and thought how happy they were. Water made the difference. All the difference in the world.

It was totally dark when she came out, her robe wrapped tightly about her. "Should I light the lamp?" she asked.

"Can if you want," he said. "Why don't you sit here a while?"

The chair creaked as she put her weight into it. Then she said: "Jim, the tree would have died if it hadn't rained, wouldn't it?"

"I think so," he said. "But it wasn't supposed to die. I take this as a sign, Jennifer. The tree will live and prosper. Patchin was right. And I know I'm right." He reached over and took her hand. "I've got plans, big plans. One of these days there'll be grass growing in that yard, and a bathtub in the bedroom. In my hand I've got the secret, and I'm going to keep it, Jennifer. I've never been more convinced of a thing."

"Yes," she said softly. "But Jim, be careful. Be wise, Jim." Then she laughed and kissed him quickly. "I'm starving. How would you like some ham and potatoes?"

"I'd like it fine. You sure you're not too tired?"

"No, I'm not tired now. Not at all. I guess it was the bath, or the rain, or something."

"I prayed to give you strength," he said.

This alarmed her a little. She said: "I guess that was answered too, then."

He sat on the porch while she worked in the kitchen, and a pale yellow shaft of lamplight came through the open door, along with the flavors of her cooking.

Tad came back, but he had someone with him. He ran on into the house, tracking mud, and Jennifer chased him out. The boy almost knocked Fred Sales over as he bowled off the porch.

"Some rain, huh?" Sales said.

102

"Come on inside," Martin said, hobbling across the porch.

"Say, you hurt yourself?"

"I've been laid up," Martin said. "Getting better now."

Sales took the chair Martin offered and smiled at Jennifer. "That ham? Thought I smelled it as I came into the yard. I've got a nose for good cooking." His glance touched Martin, and he hesitated. "Saw your boy at the creek, so I thought I'd come on with him. Jim, it didn't do more'n sprinkle at my place. Not even enough to settle the dust. The truth is, I don't expect the creek to rise a damned bit. I can walk across it now without water comin' over my boots."

"I had a cloudburst," Martin said smugly. "Right over my place the heavens opened up and let it pour. I needed water, too."

"We all need it," Sales said, none too happy about this. "Well, your grass will be a foot high in a week. You'll fatten quickly and ship, most likely."

"I figure to sell all my stock but the bull," Martin said. "Ought to make at least four thousand clear profit."

Sales digested this glum bit of news. That was about his yearly profit, and he was three times as big. "Beats me how one man can get rain while his neighbors didn't," he said.

"It's not uncommon with a cloudburst," Jennifer said. "But the ground won't hold the water long. The grass will come up, but in a month it'll be burned up again."

"I can hand feed some," Martin said. "That well I've been diggin' is full of water."

"The hell!" Sales said. "I'd like to have a look at that."

They went out, Martin carrying the lantern, and they stood there, looking at the dark water.

"The strangest thing I ever saw," Sales said softly. "Why don't the ground soak it up?" He turned and started back to the house. As he approached the door, he stopped. "That the tree I heard about?" He took the lantern from Martin and held it high. Then he walked around it and examined it carefully. The leaves were again slick and green and healthy. "Can't say as I've ever seen anything like it," Sales admitted. "It must take a lot of water."

"I've got water now," Martin said.

Jennifer came out. "Supper's on the table. Fred, will you stay and have something?"

"Thank you, I will. You know, Jim, I'd like to get a shoot off this. My wife loves trees, and there's nary a one on the place."

The thought sent a chill through Jim Martin. He said: "We'll see, Fred. Come on in to supper."

The talk during the meal was general, and Sales steered clear of mentioning either the tree or water. After he had wiped his plate clean, he slid back his chair.

"It's impolite to eat and run, but I ought to get back." Then he frowned. "Beats me about that well holdin' water like that. Well, it was a freak rain anyway. It'll never happen again." He thought a moment, then laughed. "Jim, it's a good thing you stopped shootin' that danged cannon. If it'd rained then, folks would have put you down as an Injun medicine man." He went out and stepped through the mud to his horse. Mounting he said: "This was a damned peculiar storm," and rode out.

Martin waited a moment, then went into the house. Jennifer was heating water for Tad's bath, and he was sulking about it. She took his grimy overalls outside and dropped them in a pail of water.

When she came back in, Jim Martin said: "I prayed for that rain, and I got it. Yes sir, I prayed for it. Wonder what Sales would think if he knew about that, and the tree."

"He acted odd," Jennifer said. "He wondered how much creek water was poured on those roots."

"Well, he didn't say anything."

"Because he wasn't sure," she pointed out. "Jim, do you know how much water that tree takes now?"

He thought a bit, then shook his head.

"Three barrels a day," she said softly. "Jim, I know you believe, and I don't want to take that away from you, but I want you to know that I don't like that tree. I don't like the power it has over you."

"Now, you're imagining things," he said. "Go on, give the boy his bath."

# Chapter Eleven

It seemed to Jim Martin that he could sit his horse and actually see the tallow build on his cattle. The grass was up and thicker than he could remember it, and he figured he'd be ready to ship in another two and a half to three weeks. His leg was better, nearly healed, and from dawn to dark Martin and the boy gathered stock, driving them in close for one big, final gather. They'd have to brand the calves. He figured two days for that and another day dickering with the buyer in Morgan Tanks. Then, with the money in the bank, he could start pushing down another well, with hired labor this time. Martin's only regret was that he was not overstocked. If he'd have more beef to fatten, there would be more to sell. Well, he decided, he'd have to be satisfied this time. There was water still in the well, and he would have another sunk, a deeper one, by the time this one went dry.

Fred Sales was a generous neighbor, if only for appearance's sake, for he loaned one of his riders to Jim Martin for the push to Morgan Tanks. Tad rode drag while Martin and Sales's man rode flank, and later that afternoon Jennifer came in with the wagon. Martin wanted to celebrate.

The pleased cattle buyer made the tally, wrote his check, and Martin deposited it in the bank. Kinred stayed open an hour and a half later than usual, just as a favor. And afterward Martin and his wife went to the store and, while Jennifer shopped, Martin smoked a cigar and looked very pleased. He insisted that she buy some new dresses and the boy some clothes, and they bought a new lamp for the kitchen table. When they left the store, the wagon was loaded. Tad sat on top of it all, eating some sugarhards, the first candy he had ever tasted.

The two laborers arrived early the next morning and digging began on the new well. For a site Martin chose a spot twenty yards on the other side of the first well and, while the hole grew deeper, Martin turned his attention to the tree and the proper care of it. He was a happier man, and much of the strain left his face, and his confidence was monumental. The laborers, after digging two weeks and shoring as they dug, believed him totally insane for putting all this work and money into a dry hole. It cost him four dollars a day, plus lumber, and that had to be shipped in.

The scorching sun burned up the grass that had been so green, but Martin could not summon a concern about this. When his well came in, he could make the grass green again. The banker drove out one day and had a look at the work. He seemed disturbed because Martin was putting so much money into the dry hole. Then the laborers hit sandstone at seventy-two feet and quit. The banker and everyone else said that Jim Martin would wake up now. He couldn't dig through rock.

The next day Martin went to town and took the stage to Rock Springs. There he caught the weekly train and went to Kansas City, and he was gone a week. Returning to Morgan Tanks, he stopped in Herb Manners's place and bought a round of drinks for everyone, remarked about the pleasant trip he had had, then went home, leaving them as puzzled as when he had left town. The mystery ended when four wagons came through Morgan

Tanks, loaded with a well drilling rig, pipe, laborers, a windmill, and a pump. They paused only long enough to ask directions to Jim Martin's place.

A steam rig was erected on Martin's place, and the drilling went on from dawn to dark. A casing was sunk, and the drill went deeper, and the driller kept examining the muck that came up. Four days of this then the engineer leaned on the whistle and tooted like a man gone mad. Martin raced out to see what had happened, then he stopped and stared at the ground and the small rush of clear, sweet water that came up.

"You'll have to pump her," the driller said.

"I'll pump," Martin said, and the laborers began to erect the windmill. The blades were huge, nearly fourteen feet across, a full dozen of them, heavy tin and deeply curved, powerful enough to pump water in the vaguest of breezes.

In two days the rig was finished, and by that time Martin had three huge galvanized tanks placed near the well, fed by three pipes, and the tanks were filling rapidly. All night long the mill pumped, powered by the breeze, and in the morning it all but died, barely turning in the whiff of air motion it caught sixty feet above the ground. Tad loved the windmill, climbing to the top platform and sitting there by the hour, watching the crank turn, the pump rod go slowly up and down, bringing water each time it rose — clear, cool water.

Fred Sales stayed away as long as he could, but his curiosity was too strong to be long denied. Charlie Goddard rode over, but he viewed the rig from a comfortable distance. Sales, however, studied it at length and even climbed to the top, looking for the first time at the full vast sweep of the land. It was enormous from that height.

The driller explained everything to Sales. "There's a pool under here," he said. "Likely you've got something on your place."

"I was thinking that," Sales said. "How much did this cost, Jim?"

"Nearly eight hundred dollars."

"My, that's a lot of money." He was a bit stunned at the cost, but the water gushing out of the pipes took the edge off it. Yet he was smart enough to know that several hundred of that price had gone for transportation and, since Jim Martin had absorbed it, Sales thought he ought to take advantage of it.

"You suppose you could drill on my place?"

"Sure," the driller said. "I'm through here." He thought for a moment. "I could be at your place by daybreak."

"Good enough," Sales said. He looked enviously at the well then laughed. "By God, it's better than gold, Jim."

"It is at that, isn't it?"

They walked together to Sales's horse. "Talked to my wife about the tree," he said. "I'd like to get a shoot from you, Jim."

"Hell, I wasn't thinking of letting any go just now," Martin said. "The fact is, I'm planting a few more myself." He pointed to several places on the other side of the house. "Trees make a place real homey. Maybe in the spring, Fred."

"All right," Sales said and mounted his horse. After another long look at the well he said: "Damn, I can see that on my place now. It's worth the money and then some."

Martin watched him ride out, and Jennifer came to

the porch and stood there. She said: "What's this about planting another tree?"

"Hmm, well, I thought that since one gave me water, I'd plant a few more and get more water. Can't you see that all green out there, acres of it, with fat Herefords grazing there?"

"Jim, I don't want you to plant another tree."

"Now, we've gone through that before," Martin said.

"Yes, and it isn't settled," she said. "Jim, what are you going to do about giving Sales a shoot?"

Martin's face turned somber. "I'm not goin' to give him any, that's what." He chuckled. "He'll sink a well and get dust, that's what he'll do. You think I'm going to tell him about the tree? Hell, he'd laugh at me. You've got to believe, Jennifer. You believe, and it'll work."

He left her then and walked over to the driller. Martin wanted a two-inch pipe run from the well to the tree, with a gate valve on the end so he could control the water. The driller thought he had lost his mind, but he was never a man to refuse a job or lose pay for it. The pipe was installed, then they packed up and moved across the creek to Fred Sales's place.

Martin did not go over to see Sales for a week. He had things of his own to do. He enjoyed going into Morgan Tanks because the well had changed everything for him, not only his financial potential but it had changed the attitudes of the people. They no longer looked upon him as a crackpot who fired cannons to get rain. Of course he took the cannon back and put it in the courthouse yard, but Wiggins, who lived north of town, borrowed it and began shooting. Martin's Chinese powder finally arrived, and he promptly sold it to Wiggins for almost twice what he paid for it.

In Martin's mind there was no doubt that things were on the upturn and that he couldn't lose now. He bought a suit of clothes, leaving his old things in the trash can behind the general store and, when he went to the bank, Kinred saw him coming and came to the door to meet him, offering him a cigar and a light and a chair by the desk behind the wickets.

"Heard about the well," Kinred said. Then he laughed. "For a time you had me worried, pouring all that money in the ground. But then I always said you knew what you were doing, Jim. I knew that someday you'd come into it."

"Is my credit any good?" Martin asked.

"Good? Why, it's golden. How much do you want?"

"Nine hundred," Martin said. "I want to restock now and hire a hand or two. Nine hundred ought to do it."

Kinred made some rapid calculations. "Jim, take a financier's advice and borrow fifteen hundred. You've got the water and some money in your account, so you ought to stock heavy, hand feed, then sell off while the market's good. A man in your position can buy stock that needs fattening, hold them for ninety days, and clean up."

Martin shook his head. "I mean to do that all right, but I want to hold a little cash in reserve. I might want to put down another well or two."

This was too much of a gamble for the banker. "Jim, you've got one. Be satisfied with it."

"Sales is sinking one now," Martin said. "I just thought I'd mention it."

"You may have started something around here," Kinred said. "But water's where you find it, and you were lucky."

"I guess you could say that," Martin admitted. "Put the nine hundred in my account, and I'll sign the note."

This formality took only a few minutes, and Martin marveled at it, for sixty days ago he couldn't have borrowed a hundred dollars on his place. Now, with a working well, it was worth at least ten thousand, and whoever bought it at that price would consider it a bargain.

The cattle buyer was not in his office, so Martin went to Herb Manners's place for a drink and some conversation. Manners held up his hands and insisted that the first one was on the house in honor of the most prosperous cattleman on the flats.

"Well, not quite yet," Martin said, "although I thank you for the drink." He downed it, then adjusted his celluloid collar, and brushed at some imaginary dust on the front of his coat. "Herb, you still got the door locked to Charlie Goddard?"

"You damned right. I hear he had the dt's once because he couldn't get a bottle."

"You ought to let up on him a little," Martin said. "Just a suggestion. I ain't tellin' you how to run your business." He turned his head as a horseman came down the street.

"Speak of the devil," Herb Manners said and swatted flies with his towel.

Martin walked to the door and stood there, watching Goddard dismount by the store. Then Martin walked that way, arriving as Goddard ducked under the hitch rack. He saw Martin and stopped, backing up a step until he came against the tie rail.

"I'm not lookin' for trouble," he said.

Martin smiled. "Charlie, I thought we'd already had our trouble. Ain't it about time we buried the hatchet?"

"You want to?"

"Sure," Martin said. "How long you think I'll hold a grudge?"

There was relief in Goddard's face, and he started to thrust out his hand, only he drew it back still unsure of himself.

"You ought to come out and see my well," Martin said. "And bring the missus and Pete. We can use the company."

"That's neighborly of you," Goddard said. "Jim, I'm sorry as hell about the dog. That's the truth now. I'm sorry and glad. You know, I ain't had a drink since the fight. That ain't been easy, but a man can't ride to Rock Springs when he gets a thirst. So if I hadn't let my meanness out on the dog, we'd never have fought, and Manners would never have cut me off like he has."

Martin laughed and thumped him on the shoulder. "They'll make a sober man out of you yet, Charlie." Then he walked on down the street to the cattle buyer's office.

Hansgen was from Texas originally, and he had a lean Texas look about him. Ten years before he had worked cattle for the Bar-T, and then he went north, fell into a high-stake card game, and ended up with enough to go into the buying end. He had enough shrewdness to stay with it and show a profit.

He was standing by the big window when Martin came in. Hansgen said: "You makin' up with Charlie Goddard?"

Martin shrugged. "Can't go through life with my tail cocked."

"You might make up with Charlie, but he'll never make up with you, inside where it counts." Hansgen tapped Martin on the chest with his finger. "He's like a mean horse, never be able to do anything with him. So you watch him, huh?"

Martin laughed, not taking Hansgen seriously. "All right, I'll watch him."

"Good. I don't want the prosperous citizens killed off." He rubbed his hands together briskly. "I expect you're buying today, not selling."

"Yep. What have you got?"

# Chapter Twelve

The speculative cattle business suited Jim Martin. He could buy cheap from water-starved ranchers, men who had to sell something between seasons to make ends meet, then fatten the cattle for ninety days, and sell at double the purchase price. It was a sure-fire business. Barring some catastrophe that was an act of God, such as a hole opening up in the ground and swallowing his herd, it could not fail.

Martin had painters add three coats of white to his house but not before the carpenters went to work, building on three more rooms and extending the porch around all four sides. He spent most of his time supervising the activity, and with two hands on the payroll he had the leisure to pursue a few pleasures.

One of them was to ride over to Fred Sales's place and watch the driller sink the well. They were down a hundred and nine feet now, and there was no sign of water or much hope of getting any. Sales was a man torn between two horrible possibilities, and he was unable to reach a decision. He could spend more money and sink another well or go deeper and risk losing it all. Or he could abandon what he had already done and lose his investment.

"God damn it, Jim," he said. "You've got to help me."

They were sitting on Sales's porch. Martin had his sixty-dollar boots cocked up on the railing, and his thirty-dollar hat lay on the floor. Edith Sales came out with a tray of drinks of lemonade and a bowl of sugar. She sat down beside her husband and shared his worry.

They waited for Jim Martin to say something. It would be important for he had succeeded where others had failed, and they wanted to know how he did it.

"Well, I wouldn't stop drilling," Martin said smoothly. "Fred, it's going to cost a little money, no matter how you look at it. You've still got the creek to carry you through, and the rains will come in another week or so. It's getting to be that time of the year."

"This is going to be a dry year," Sales said dully. "Look at the sky. You ever see it this bright and clear this far into the season?" He shook his head. "It wouldn't surprise me if we got no rain at all." He spread his hands. "How the hell can I go on drilling? I've got nearly three thousand in the bank right now, just enough to carry me through the winter, hand feeding. But not enough to drill and hand feed. Which way am I going to turn?"

Martin pondered the problem a moment, then said: "How many head do you have, Fred?"

"Fifteen hundred. A little more, maybe. Why?"

"I'll buy half of 'em."

Sales seemed insulted. "You trying to break me or trying to help me? Hell, I wouldn't be able to ship and show a profit in the spring if I sold off half of what I owned. It'd put me back a year because I can't pour water on the ground and make the grass grow like you can." He shook his head violently. "I can't do that, Jim. To hell with the well. I'll just have to make up the loss somewhere."

"You suit yourself," Martin said. "But remember, you thought I was crazy, sinking everything in the hope of getting water." He reached over and tapped Sales on the leg. "But keep in mind one thing. You sell off half your herd and sink another well in some other spot, and you get water, you'll be able to buy a thousand head of cattle."

A rider came from the direction of the creek, and Sales squinted. "Ain't that your boy?"

"Yes," Martin said.

He watched the boy approach, riding his new pony, and he felt proud, because the boy was happy, and because he had finally made the boy happy. To hell with what the philosophers said. A man could make a lot more people happy with money than without it. Tad waved and rode up to the porch, flinging off, then tying the pony.

"My, that is a pretty pony," Edith Sales said. "Care for some lemonade?"

The boy looked at his father to see if he should and, when Martin nodded slightly, the boy accepted the glass, perching himself on the porch railing and dangling his legs. He wore jeans, a bright green cotton shirt, and a belt with a five dollar silver buckle. His boots were new and stiff with bright metal buttons set in patterns.

"Keeping you busy, Tad?" Sales asked.

"I keep the tree watered," Tad said. "Sure is growing."

"Yes," Sales said softly. "I'll bet you keep busy." He looked at Martin. "Is it all right if the boy stays for supper?"

"Hmm, I guess. You mind your manners, Tad."

"Yes, Pa."

Martin sat there a moment longer, listening to the steam rig puff and thump, then he got out of the chair. "Think about what I said, Fred. I'll hold the offer open a week."

"I'll surely think about it," Sales said and walked with

Martin to his horse. Then he stood there while Martin rode out. Coming back to his chair on the porch, he settled himself, then said: "Tad, I've missed having you around."

"There sure is a lot to do," Tad said. "Ma's getting curtains and new dishes from Chicago. Furniture too, on account of them new rooms."

"I'll have to come over and see that," Edith said. "Ask your mother when, Tad."

"Any time'd be all right," he said.

Sales scratched his cheek. "Tad, why don't you run over to the rig and see how they're comin' along? Do a favor for an old man."

"All right," Tad said and scooted off the porch. He got on his pony and rode toward the pasture behind the barn.

Edith Sales said: "Why did you ask him to stay for supper? You know I don't like to cook for people."

"You ever think about how a kid will talk when his old man won't?"

She looked steadily at him. "What are you thinking, Fred?"

"Right now not much. But it won't hurt to pump him a little for something besides water." He tightened his lips and looked out onto the shimmering flats, at his grass burned until it was almost gone. "There's a lot I don't understand, Edith. A mighty lot."

"Are you going to sell to Martin?"

Sales shrugged. "He's got water, and I've got a dry hole in the ground. He gambled, and I hesitate. Maybe he's right. A man might have to take the big plunge before he gets anything. We'll see, Edith."

"What do you think the boy can tell you?"

"More about Jim Martin's affairs than I know now," Sales said.

Sales was alone on the porch when Tad came back. He sat down in the chair Edith had vacated and said: "No water, Mister Sales. It's still a dry hole."

"Afraid of that," Sales said. "Well, come on in the house." He slapped the boy on the leg and went on in. Edith was in the kitchen, and they washed at the sink, pouring water from a bucket. Sales still had to haul his water, but not as far as Martin had once hauled it.

Edith Sales wasn't much of a cook, not as good as Jennifer Martin, and Tad ate the half-cooked potatoes, the steak that had been fried too long, and the vegetable fresh out of a can. Neither by word nor sign did he let on that this was not the best he had ever eaten.

"Your dad sure is lucky," Sales said, while he poured his coffee. "I mean, getting water the way he did. Yes, sir, really lucky. Some men have to fight hard for what they want, but your dad hit it lucky."

"My pa makes his own luck," Tad said flatly. "Nothin' come easy for him."

"Well, I expect you to be loyal," Sales said soothingly, "but a man has to look at it a little differently, Tad. Your dad was lucky, and that's all there is to it." He spread his hands in a final gesture. "What else is there? He gambled and won."

"Pa always knew he'd get water," Tad said.

Sales glanced significantly at his wife then covered it by reaching for the pie she had baked. "Come on, let's have some pie." He put a wedge on Tad's plate. "It's funny, you saying a thing like that, Tad. I mean, about your dad knowin' he'd get water. Son, no man knows what's in the ground."

"Pa knew because he put water there," Tad said. He was on the defensive now. Sales was attacking the most important person the boy knew, and he resented it. His conscience would not allow him to let this go unchallenged.

Sales managed to laugh, and Edith smiled, but good humor was only on their lips; their eyes were hard and bright and guarded. "How could a man put water in the ground, Tad?" He chuckled. "I guess you're imagining this, huh?"

"I am not," Tad said. "Pa did."

Waiting for him to say more, Sales realized that the boy was naturally too closed mouth. He responded only to a prodding. "Your pa fed you some hot air, boy," Sales said. "He's just like any other man. Maybe a little dumber, but like anyone else."

"He's not dumb! He's smarter than you, or anyone else," Tad snapped. "He got water, didn't he?"

"Well, I'm from Missouri, Tad. I've got to be shown a thing before I believe it."

"There's nothing to show," Tad said warily.

Sales shrugged. "All right then, forget it. You tried to sell me a hot air story and, when it didn't work, you're backing down. I'll bet your pa wouldn't be proud of you, if he knew how easily you backed down."

"I ain't backin' down! I can prove what I say!"

"That's all Fred asked," Edith said. "A little proof."

The boy looked from one to the other and was torn between desire to defend his father's name and a natural inclination to keep family business in the family. "It's the tree that brought water," Tad said. "Pa planted the tree and kept it alive, and God gave us water."

Sales and his wife looked at each other, then Edith

said: "Tad, don't you know it's wrong to lie?"

"I ain't lyin'!" He pushed back his chair, deserting his half-eaten pie, then ran out of the house. Sales started to rise to follow him then thought better of it. He sat back down again.

"What do you make of it?" Edith asked.

"Don't know," Sales said. "But it'll take some lookin' into."

"The boy was lying, of course," she said.

Sales laughed hollowly. "You're a fool. That boy wouldn't know what a lie was. Neither would his father. No, he told the truth. Somehow Jim Martin planted that damned tree and got water."

"Now you're the fool," Edith said, "if you expect me to believe that fairy tale." She got up and started to clean off the table. "I guess when some men are squeezed hard enough, they're ready to grab at anything. Well, not me."

"Don't be too smart for your own good," Sales said. "I was in Herb's place the night Goddard told Martin about that old bastard in Rock Springs who could make rain. We'd heard about him, but all thought it was hot air, so Goddard thought he'd make a joke of it and send Martin on a snipe hunt. Well, it could have turned out differently than we figured. Martin came back with this damned tree. I can't figure out where else he got it. And he watered it from my creek, damn it, so I guess I've got an interest in it." He slapped the table hard, then got up. "If Martin's got onto something, I want part of it. It's my due."

"You think he's just going to hand it to you?"

"No, but I'll get a tree just like it." He walked to the front door and yelled for one of his hands to come to the house. When the man walked up, Sales said: "Hoby,

121

saddle a horse and ride to Goddard's place. Tell him I want to see him right away."

"Sure, Mister Sales."

Sales turned back into the house, rubbing his hands. Edith was at the sink, and she looked at him, a question in her eyes. "What good is that going to do, Fred?"

"Martin got a tree, didn't he? Well, I guess Goddard can too."

"I don't want him around," she said. "I know I crossed you once, but I've changed my mind. I don't want him around, Fred."

"I can use Charlie," Sales said. "Let me do it my way, will you? He's just right for the job."

Tad returned home before sundown, and Martin was surprised to see him. When the boy had put up his horse, he came directly to the house. Martin asked: "Supper over already? A man ought to stay a while afterward and be friendly." He bent his head, looked at the boy, then cupped his hand under Tad's chin and raised his head so he could look into his eyes. "You've got a sour face. Something go wrong?" He put his arm around the boy's shoulders. "Come on, sit down and tell me about it."

"He said you were dumb, Pa."

"Fred said that?"

Tad nodded. "He said a lot of other things and that I lied when I said you knew you'd get water. You really knew, didn't you, Pa?"

"Yes, I really knew." He looked at the boy, studied him, and knew that Tad had told Sales all about the tree, still he had to ask to be sure beyond a doubt. "You told him about the tree?"

"Yes, Pa. I didn't want to, but he thought I was lyin'. Did I do wrong, Pa?"

"No," Jim said softly. "You did what you thought you had to do." He reached out and gave the boy a thump on the shoulder. "Go on and play a while, but take a bath before you go to bed."

"This is Wednesday, Pa!"

"Take a bath twice a week now that we've got water," Martin said and went into the house. Jennifer was sitting in the parlor, reading. She put the magazine down when her husband came in.

"I heard you talking. Did Tad come home?"

Martin nodded.

"He didn't stay long. I hope he wasn't impolite."

"He told Fred Sales about the tree," Martin said. He stood there, frowning, thinking. "Hard to tell whether Fred will believe it or not, but he'll look into it anyway. Think I'll hitch up the wagon and go to Rock Springs. I wanted to get three or four more shoots from old man Patchin anyway."

"Tonight?" she asked. Then she got up and came over to him, putting her hands lightly on his chest. "Jim, you've never been a selfish man. If Sales wants to plant a tree, then let him." She laughed uneasily. "Now see? You've got me half believing about that tree. Sales will get water any time now."

Martin shook his head. "Not without the tree." He took a cigar from the humidor, nipped off the end, then struck a match. "I talked to Fred about buying half his stock. I think he'll go for it, now that he's got drilling fever. But he'll end up with his place full of dry holes."

"He can't afford that," Jennifer said.

"Not unless he sells off," Martin said. He looked steadily

123

at her. "I've given some thought to expansion, Jennifer. Sales can't quit, and he can't go on. When he gets tired of it all, I'll buy him out."

"You want to break him, Jim? Why?"

His eyes narrowed, and his voice was like a gentle wind. "Because I can see cattle with my brand on them from horizon to horizon. This house will be sixteen rooms, a landmark for seventy miles, and we'll have a maid pours your tea and cooks the meals." He put his arms around her and held her against him. "There won't be a thing you won't have, Jennifer. And when I snap my fingers, people will jump to do what I say has to be done. The boy can go to a fine school, and we can have some more kids, and they'll never know what it means to go dirty, wear one pair of overalls all year, and never taste a bite of candy until they're nearly ten."

He released her then and went to the closet for his coat and his shotgun. He smiled when he looked at it, for it was about all that remained of the old things.

"I'll be back in four days," he said, then went to her and kissed her.

# Chapter Thirteen

Martin took an empty barrel with him and a dozen burlap sacks, all stowed in the back of the wagon. Tad wanted to go along, but Martin said no and drove off into the gathering darkness, taking the town road. As soon as a full darkness came, he left the road and cut across the flats, enduring the bone-jarring irregularities.

Off the road this way, he figured he could travel to Rock Springs without being seen by anyone, and traveling light he could make Patchin's place by dawn. In Martin's mind there was a question of what he would say to Patchin. He wasn't sure the old man would even remember him, and he wasn't sure what he would do about the tree Patchin had. There wasn't any way, really, to prevent Patchin from giving Fred Sales a shoot off the tree. Then Sales would have everything Jim Martin had, only he wouldn't really have to work for it at all, not the way Martin had worked.

There was no fairness to this, the way Martin saw it. One man had it good, and now stood to have it a lot better, while the other had endured poverty and back-breaking labor. To his way of thinking, Martin felt deserving of his reward, while Fred Sales was not.

It was the longest night Jim Martin had ever known, for he could not give his mind rest at all. He was glad to see the first pink rush of dawn, glad to see the smudge of Rock Springs on the horizon. He altered course slightly and arrived at Patchin's fallen-down place just as a full sun spread brightness across the land.

Martin put the team and wagon in Patchin's dilapidated barn. No one would ever notice it there, should anyone pass this way. He walked then to the mud house and, as he approached, he thought it even more fallen down than before. The glass had been broken from all the windows, and the door hung askew on the hinges.

A trickle of water still oozed from the pipe, and the tree was healthy and leafy, but it looked more gnarled than Martin remembered. He could not help but think that it was plagued with some illness from which there was no recovery.

At the door Martin knocked and listened to the hollow echo of the sound. Then he stepped inside, and a rat darted between his legs, startled into leaving his dark corner.

"Patchin?" He put out the question and got no answer at all.

Martin looked around the room. Dust lay thick and undisturbed, and he knew that no one had been here for months. Dishes lay on the table, and a skillet was on the stove, the grease hardened in the bottom. Patchin's clothes lay scattered about, but the mice and rats had been in them, leaving them full of holes and useless.

He went outside and stood in the sunlight, wondering what he should do. Martin didn't want to go to town and look for Patchin. He didn't want anyone remembering that he had been asking for the old man. This thought gave him a moment of inner reflection, then he understood why he had come here, to destroy the tree so that Fred Sales could never grow one like it. The time had come when there could only be one tree — his own. Martin went to the barn to see if Patchin had an axe.

He found one deeply imbedded in a block of wood and,

when he withdrew it, he found the blade sharp and clean and free of rust. There was also a saw, greased and hanging on a post. He took these to the tree and removed his coat.

The tree was harder than anything he had ever sunk an axe in, and the sweat poured down his face, soaking his white shirt as he made the back undercut. Martin worked until his arm and back muscles were aflame, then he rested a bit and began his saw cut. Back and forth he drew the saw, watching the white shavings build into a pile on both sides of the tree.

Noon came and passed, and the cut went deeper, striking at the life of the tree, and he felt it shake slightly, and the leaves rustled over his head, still he sawed on. When it fell, it did so slowly, as though trying to stay erect. It crashed amid broken branches and left a tall, ragged shard of wood on the stump from the final, wrenching parting. Martin stood there, dirty, sweating, looking at his work, then he picked up the axe and saw and returned them to the barn. He left the axe imbedded in the same block of wood, just as he found it, then he greased the saw and rehung it on the pole.

There were no young shoots to choose from even though he searched for them. Then he supposed the tree was like a man, reaching a certain age after which reproduction is impossible. Martin was disappointed, but then he figured that his own young tree would soon provide shoots for replanting.

Going back to the barn, he found his team and wagon, and climbed aboard. As he turned out of the yard, he took one final look at the tree and noticed then that the trickle of water from the rusty pipe had all but died out to occasional dripping. A sudden and thorough fear charged through Jim Martin, and he knew he had stopped the water when he destroyed the tree.

The late afternoon sun suddenly lost its warmth, and he hurriedly drove out of the yard, pointing the team south again across the vast sweep of land. Martin's one thought was to return to his own place as quickly as he could. Two more hours and it would be dark again. He could stop then, sleep a little, and press on, arriving home in the early morning. The hands would never question him, and he could tell Jennifer something that would satisfy her. Or perhaps she wouldn't question him at all when he came back without some new shoots to plant. She didn't want him to plant any more trees, and her relief might lead her to believe that he had changed his mind. Anyway, it was just something he'd have to cover when he came to it, but he hoped he wouldn't have to lie to her. He'd never done that and just thinking about it bothered him.

At dusk he stopped the wagon and laid down on the prairie and slept a while, but it wasn't a good sleep, and he woke often, sweating, turning, unable to find a comfortable position. After several hours of this he got up and moved off, not much rested at all.

It occurred to Martin that he ought to stop in Morgan Tanks, to be seen there in the saloon or someplace. Everyone would think he had come in from his place. Calculating miles to go and time, he figured he could raise the town around nine-thirty, which was early enough for some of the stores to be still open. He slapped the team to a brisker pace.

Traveling on the Rock Springs-Morgan Tanks Road was easier and faster and, since there wasn't much traffic on it save the once-a-week stage, Martin didn't think he would meet anyone. And if he did, it would be dark, and he could go on quickly and in that way remain unidentified.

Feeling thus, he was surprised when a horseman loomed up before him, and without thinking Martin reined in. The horseman came closer, then Charlie Goddard said: "Well, for Christ's sake, Jim Martin!"

"What you doin' out here, Charlie?"

"On my way to Rock Springs," Goddard said. "Say, you got any tobacco? I ran out a few miles back."

Martin had cigars in his pocket, but he said: "I'm fresh out myself, Charlie. What you goin' to Rock Springs for? Gettin' thirsty again?"

"Naw, I've swore off the booze," Goddard said. His horse stirred, and he kneed him around so that he faced the same direction as Jim Martin "Sales is starting a new hole tomorrow. He thinks he's goin' to get water for sure this time." Goddard smiled. Martin could see the gleam of his teeth. "After he's through with the driller, I'm goin' to have him sink a well, too. And I'll get water."

"Here's wishin' you luck," Martin said dryly.

"You think we won't do it, huh?" He laughed. "Your kid kind of spilled the beans, didn't he?"

"Kids talk a lot. You can't put store by it."

"Sure they do. They say what they hear over the kitchen table." He shifted in the saddle and placed his hands flat on the pommel. "I meant it to be a joke, telling you about Patchin. Maybe I ought to listen to myself a little better, huh?"

"Either that or don't talk so much," Martin said. He bent closer and peered at Charlie Goddard. "You wearin' a gun?"

129

"Free country, ain't it? Fred loaned it to me. You never know who you're goin' to meet on the road." He had the weapon stuck in the waistband of his jeans, and he drew it, flourishing it in no particular direction. "Pretty nice, huh? I used to have a Forty-Five, too, but I sold it one time when I got dry."

"Better put it up before you shoot your horse," Martin said.

"Oh, I can handle it," Goddard said. "You're lucky I didn't have this when you jumped me in town. You wouldn't be here now." He held the gun in his hand but crossed his arms and leaned forward in the saddle. "Your woman took a shot at me. I ought to take one at you and even it up."

The tone warned Martin. He said: "I guess Hansgen was right."

"Right about what?"

"You're just a mean son of a bitch," Martin said and cast himself off the wagon.

He meant to sweep Goddard clear of the horse, go clean over with him, but Goddard shied the horse away just in time, and they fell between horse and wagon. Startled, Goddard's horse galloped away, and both men rolled in the road, trying to take possession of the gun.

Martin grabbed it around the frame and cylinder and, as long as he held it that way, Charlie Goddard could not get it cocked. With their free hands each tried to knock the other out, but they could not land a decent blow. Martin took Goddard's pummeling on the neck and shoulders, all the time concentrating on his grip on the gun.

Goddard rolled, trying to get on top of Martin, and Martin rolled with him, letting Goddard's surge of power

130

carry them completely over. Martin ended astraddle of Goddard. Sweating, his hand started to slip on the gun, and Martin felt the cylinder rotate as Goddard eared the hammer back. With his free hand he grabbed the barrel and pressed the muzzle against Goddard's breast just as he pulled the trigger.

Kicking like an unbroken horse, Goddard jerked and strangled, and Martin hastily got off him and stood there, watching him die. The muzzle blast had set fire to Goddard's shirt, and Martin threw some dust on it, putting it out.

Goddard was dead, and Martin stood there, wondering what to do. The man's horse had run off, probably heading home for the barn. Putting Goddard in the wagon and taking him back to Morgan Tanks would open the door to a lot of questions, and Martin didn't want to answer any.

This was Thursday. A stage would be through next Tuesday. They'd find him and that would be soon enough. He thought about picking up Goddard's gun, then changed his mind. Be better if it stayed with him. Besides, it was Fred Sales's gun.

Climbing onto his wagon, Martin pushed on, riding round shouldered and trying to decide whether he should tell what he knew and hope everyone believed him, or keep quiet and pretend to know nothing. By the time he reached Morgan Tanks, he had decided.

He parked the wagon in front of Herb Manners's place and went in. There wasn't much of a crowd, this being the middle of the week, and the men standing by the bar were all merchants, having a beer before going home. Herb drew a beer as Martin came up to the bar.

"I can use that," Martin said. "That ride from the place

never gets shorter or less dusty."

"Odd time for you to be in town," Herb said.

Martin shrugged. "Got a lot to do tomorrow, so I thought I'd spend the night at the hotel, buy what I want, and be home by noon." He looked at the string of watchful merchants standing there. "Make sense to you?"

"Sure does," one said, and the others murmured their agreement.

"I'd like to buy a round," Martin said. "Herb, uncork some of that Saint Louis whiskey." He dropped a twenty dollar gold piece on the bar, and the merchants all looked at it.

There was about Martin the air of prosperity. He had the Midas touch, and they liked to be with him for a little of it might rub off. He represented a great deal to these men for he had come into water, and the revenue of the town would increase because of it. Each man there was silently figuring and refiguring just about how much he could take home for himself.

"That place of yours is a landmark," the harnessmaker said. "One of these days I want to take my wife out and have a look."

"You're more than welcome," Martin said. "Which reminds me, I want to talk to you about a saddle, a roper. A little higher in the pommel than usual and with full, square skirts. You got a good tree?"

"The best. Drop around at the shop before you leave in the morning."

"I'll do that."

Herb had dealt the whiskey, and each man lifted his glass, offering a salute to Martin's good luck, his health, his continued prosperity. He stayed and talked a little, telling them something of his plans. Then he left and

132

started down the street to the hotel, hoping the kitchen would still be open so he could get a meal.

Hansgen was in the dining room and, when he saw Jim Martin come in, he motioned him over to his table. The waiter poked his head out of the kitchen to see who had come in, and Martin gave him his order.

Finished eating, Hansgen was on his second cup of coffee, but he decided to have a third so he could sit and talk. "I got word today that there's a man over in Rock Springs who wants to sell a hundred and thirty head of shorthorns. You interested, Jim?"

"Sure. Every little bit helps."

"What are you shooting for? A thousand head?"

"I think I can hand feed fifteen hundred," Martin said. "But I'll have to put on a few more hands."

"Well, you're in a position to carry a payroll now," Hansgen said. "But speaking of shooting, Goddard was in town this afternoon, and he had a pistol stuck in his belt."

"So?"

Hansgen shrugged. "So I thought he might be hoping to meet you. I don't trust him, Jim."

"You don't trust anybody," Martin said jokingly. "It's a good way to be in your business, but I think you're wrong about Charlie. I offered him friendship, and I think he'll accept it. Bill, I just can't hold anything against a man. Call it a weakness if you want."

"Naw, I wouldn't do that," Hansgen said. "But I want to tell you something . . . and take it right. You're on the upgrade now, Jim, and a lot of people you used to call friend are going to sharpen their sights for you. Funny how they figure it, but a poor man is supposed to stay poor and, if he does make it, they feel it's right to take it away from him." He turned his head when the waiter appeared. "Here's your supper." He got up and replaced his chair at the table. "I'll get those cattle for you, but remember what I said."

He went out, and Martin finished his supper, topping it off with a wedge of peach pie. Cal McKitrich looked in, all a part of his nightly rounds and, when he saw Jim Martin sitting there, he came over to the table.

"I haven't seen you since before your fight with Charlie," McKitrich said. He sat down across from Martin and shifted his pistol around to a more comfortable position.

"And I didn't see you during the fight," Martin said.

McKitrich laughed. "Jim, I'd have been fired if I'd butted in." He shook his head. "I was sleeping soundly in my hotel room."

"What if Charlie had been carryin' a gun?" Martin asked. "What then?"

"He wouldn't think of that," McKitrich said softly. "Jim, this isn't gun country. No money. Where there's money, there's guns. Now you take Kinred at the bank. He's got two or three guns layin' around. And Jessup at the store. You and Sales and Goddard and the rest never carry a gun because you don't need one. However, I guess that's goin' to change, and I'll be earnin' my money."

Martin frowned. "What's that mean, Cal?"

"You've got money now," McKitrich said. "Why, out there on your range there's five thousand dollars on the hoof. You think Goddard and Sales and the others ain't lookin' at that? They're lookin' hard, and they're thinkin' hard and, if they don't get much rain this winter, they're goin' to come to you for help. Sales will want you to run water to his place, and he'll remind you of the years you dipped out of his creek. And the others will have some-

134

thing too, something they want, something to remind you of what they did for you. What you goin' to say to 'em, Jim?"

"I don't know. You've left out Charlie Goddard."

"So I have. But then, Charlie's never given anyone anything in his life, so I figure he'll turn to rustlin'. Seems like I'll have to hang him one of these days." McKitrich appeared saddened by this thought. "Now, if Charlie had been a little generous, you'd be owin' him, and he wouldn't have to turn rustler. Oh, I'd bet that's how it comes out, Jim. The pattern's there, and Charlie's one for following a pattern. But what are you goin' to say to the others?"

"I guess I'll give them what they want," Martin said. "They never said no to me."

"A poor man can do that," McKitrich said, "but not a prosperous one, Jim. Give Sales or Leverett or any of the others anything, and they'll put you down as soft and start thinkin' about how much more they can take."

"I'm glad," Martin said, "that I don't have your outlook on life."

"A product of experience," McKitrich said. "The whole thing can change if Sales's dry hole turns wet." He took out his sack tobacco and rolled a cigarette. "Makes for interesting possibilities, don't it?"

"Yes," Martin said.

McKitrich got up and pushed his gun farther back on his hip. "Staying at the hotel tonight?" Martin nodded. "Well, sleep with your door locked. Charlie Goddard came in town wearing a pistol."

After he left, Martin placed fifty cents on the table and then went to the night clerk for a room. Before he used to get one of the back rooms, with a view of a littered alley, but now the clerk gave him one fronting the upper gallery with a clean look at the main street.

He was physically exhausted, yet his sleep was not deep, nor satisfying. He awoke in the morning feeling no more rested than when he had lain down. Because he had said he had come to town to shop, he dressed and took his rig to the livery and there loaded it with hay and sacks of grain. Martin was on the road home by the time most of the merchants opened their stores. He remembered then his conversation with the saddle-maker, but it would have to wait now until he made another trip.

Tad saw him approaching the house and rode to meet him. "Where's the trees, Pa?"

"Well, I decided not to get 'em. We'll take shoots off our own tree."

"There's some little ones comin' up," Tad said. He held his hand about six inches from the saddlehorn. "About that high."

"We'll give 'em a chance to grow," Martin said.

"I'm goin' to ride on and tell Ma," Tad said and flailed the pony into a gallop. Martin watched him and was immeasurably pleased with the boy and pleased with himself because he had been able to give him the things every boy should have.

Martin realized then that Cal McKitrich was right. He would fight now for what he had. Fight with a gun if he had to, and hire guns if his alone was not enough, for no one would destroy this now, not without destroying Martin first. He'd have to gain strength rapidly, he knew, grow so strong that any man would hesitate before tackling him. That was the only way for a man really to protect himself. Sales would be the first one to look longingly at him, so he'd have to clip some of the feathers from Sales's wings.

Jennifer came to the porch, drying her hands on her apron, and Martin got down and kissed her and held her as though he had been away a long time.

"Take the team to the barn," Jim told Tad, "and have Al and Skinny unload. Tell them I bought some more cattle. They ought to arrive in a week, about a hundred and thirty head."

The boy led the team away, and Jennifer took his arm, squeezing it. "Jim, what made you change your mind about the trees? Are you satisfied that you have enough now?"

"I'll have shoots of my own come spring," he said. Then he saw the shadow cross her smile, and he put his arm around her and led her into the house. "Honey, don't worry. I know what I'm doing."

"Do you really? Jim, you're wooing strange gods, and it frightens me."

"The tree?" He shook his head. "What I've done has been done before. Old man Patchin must have had his tree for years, and it didn't bring any curse on him." He laughed at her fears. "That's what you think, isn't it? That it'll bring a curse down on me? Well, it ain't so. I got water because I believed strong enough, and I've given some thought to it, indeed I have. Now that tree ain't the only thing. And one of these days I'll show you. It's what I believed that brought water in my well and nothing but dust in Sales's. And when I believe that I'm stronger than that tree, I'll take an axe and cut it down, because I won't need it any more. The tree was only to help me believe, Jennifer. It ain't everything. And a man can get stronger and believe harder, and I'll know when I'm strong enough."

"Jim, let's just say that the tree *did* bring water, and that God put it there, the tree and the water. No man is stronger than God, Jim."

He laughed and kissed her resoundingly. "You just stop worryin', you hear? I ain't gettin' into a wrestlin' match with God. No sir."

Sunday evening at sundown Marshal Cal McKitrich rode out from town and dismounted at the house. Martin heard him and walked out onto the porch.

"This is a surprise," he said. "I could even call it a pleasure, Cal." He turned his head and called to his wife. "Jennifer, the marshal's here! Bring out some coffee." He motioned to one of the chairs. "Sit a spell. We'll go inside at full dark." He waited until McKitrich sat down, then took the chair beside him. "Some changes in the place, huh?"

"None I didn't expect," McKitrich said. "Yes, you've come into your luck, Jim, and I must say it couldn't have happened to a nicer fella." He turned his head when Jennifer came out with a tray, then stood up until she sat down on the other side of Martin. There was sugar and cream for the coffee, and McKitrich was appreciative of this. "The banker don't live any better than this." He smiled at Jennifer. "You're lookin' good, Missus Martin."

"I'm feeling good," she said. "And if I get to feeling poorly, I'll go out and dump a bucket of water on the ground and take pleasure in the fact that I don't have to cry over the waste of it."

"The land's put its last wrinkle in her face," Martin said solemnly. "That's what I think. She'll never get older than she is now, and that's enough for me."

She laughed and slapped him on the leg, but she was pleased with his words.

"That's a right handsome dress you're wearin'," McKitrich said. "One from Saint Louis?"

"Yes. I keep telling Jim it's too good to wear every day, but he just laughs. I've got a romantic fool for a husband."

"Jim's luck runs to more than findin' water," McKitrich said. He started to roll a cigarette, but Martin made him put the sack tobacco away and accept one of his ten cent cigars. Between puffs McKitrich said: "Speakin' of luck, I do hope Charlie Goddard's hasn't run out on him."

"What do you mean?" Jennifer asked.

"This afternoon Missus Goddard and the boy came to see me. Seems that Charlie headed for Fred Sales's place Thursday afternoon and hasn't been seen since." McKitrich studied the tip of his cigar a moment. "I figured that maybe Herb relented, sold Charlie a bottle, and he was sleeping it off some place. But Herb swears he ain't seen Charlie since he stopped in town Thursday afternoon, late." McKitrich brushed a finger against his mustache. "I hate to go to Sales right off and ask him a lot of questions. He's feeling a little pecky since his well came a cropper, and this new hole don't look any better than the last. So I thought maybe you could give me a hand, Jim. If it ain't askin' too much."

"I'll be glad to do what I can," Martin said. "What did you have in mind?"

"I'd like to know where Goddard went after goin' to Sales's place. Whether he stayed there or went somewhere else. It occurred to me that we could ride over

139

there together and, while you talked to Fred, I could ask a few questions of the hands."

"Fine. In the morning?"

"Sure, I guess that's soon enough."

"You can stay the night here," Martin said.

"Thank you." McKitrich laughed. "Likely this will come to nothing at all, except some chasin' on our part. But it's part of the job, I guess."

"Could he have gone to Rock Springs?" Jennifer asked.

"Sure. He's gone there before. But it's a long ride for a man with no particular business there."

"He could have got too dry," Martin said. "Forty miles ain't far when there's a bottle of whiskey at the end."

"That's occurred to me," McKitrich admitted. "Well, if we don't turn up anything at Sales's place, we'll look into Rock Springs. Of course, I wouldn't ask you to make the ride. It's my job."

# Chapter Fourteen

Fred Sales was in a sour frame of mind when Martin and McKitrich rode into his yard. His greeting was short, and by his manner he indicated his desire to be left alone. Sales did not come out and ask McKitrich what he wanted, and McKitrich did not tell him. He let the conversation run a moment or two then excused himself and walked toward the corral.

When he was out of earshot, Sales said: "What the hell's the city marshal doin' on my place?"

"He stayed the night at mine," Martin said. "So I don't see what you're put out for. I had to feed him breakfast."

"Never did like the law snoopin' around," Sales said. He jammed his hands into his pockets and stood there, a deep scowl on his face. Away from the house the steam rig raised and lowered the drilling bit, and the very sound of its working seemed to annoy Sales.

"How far are you down this time?" Martin asked.

"Forty-two feet." He clenched his teeth a moment. "God damn, I'm out all that money for casing and labor, and I've got nothing to show for it except a hole that gives back an echo when you holler down it."

"Decided to go on then, huh?"

"Christ, how can I quit?" He shook his head sadly. "I'm spendin' money I can't afford to spend."

"My offer to buy seven hundred and fifty head still holds."

"Well, I might," Sales said.

"Going to be a dry winter, looks like. I don't hold out much hope for rain."

"Did you have to say that?" Sales was angry.

"Sayin' what I thought, that's all," Martin said. "If it don't rain, it ain't my fault." He looked around a moment then again came back to his point. "We could ride into town this afternoon and close the deal, Fred. Hell, this well will come in. Your luck's bound to change."

Sales stared at him. "You and I both know it ain't luck at all, Jim. I'm goin' to have me one of them trees, and I'll water it until the last drop of moisture is gone from the creek." He pointed to the drilling rig. "This time I'm going to get a gusher."

"Thought you didn't believe in rain makin'?"

"Well, I don't, but I've told you before, I've got an open mind. A man comes up with something workable, Fred Sales is right there, eyes and ears open. Yes, sir, you got to get up mighty early to get this old fox. That's why I'm selling you half my herd now, Jim. By spring, I'll have a larger herd fattened and ready for market."

"I don't see your tree," Martin said softly.

"I damn' sure said I was goin' to get one, didn't I? And when Fred Sales says a thing, it's so." He nodded curtly, a single bob of his head. "Come tomorrow I'll have it in the ground right here in the yard." He looked past Martin as McKitrich came back to the porch. "I hope you're done snoopin'," Sales snapped.

"Might be that I'm just starting," McKitrich said. "Fred, where did Charlie Goddard go when he left here?"

"Who said he was here?"

"His wife did. She said you sent a rider for him, and I just talked to the man. He said you had a job for Charlie, and he left right away."

"As a matter of fact," Sales said, "I did have a chore for Charlie. Expect he's on his way back right now."

142

"From Rock Springs?" Martin asked. McKitrich looked from one to the other, not getting the connection. "You send Charlie after a tree, Fred?"

"Yes," Sales said defensively. "By God, you don't have a monopoly on 'em, do you?"

"No," Martin said. "Well, Cal, there's your answer to where Charlie is."

"I guess," McKitrich said. "But send him home, Fred. His wife's worried."

"Drunk or sober?" Martin asked. He looked at Fred Sales and laughed. "Charlie won't get your damned tree. He'll smell the saloon, fall off the wagon, and drink his pockets empty."

Sales showed a superior smile. "I'm smarter than that. His pockets were empty when he left, and Charlie's credit ain't worth a damn."

Martin nodded. "Well, then I guess you're goin' to get water, after all, Fred."

"Yeah, and ain't you happy?"

"Let's go," McKitrich said. He stepped into the saddle and, when Martin mounted up, they turned out of the yard together. Away from the house McKitrich said: "I wasted your time, Jim. I'm sorry."

"No waste. We know where Charlie is, so we can all quit worrying."

"I'll stop in and see his wife."

McKitrich rode as far as the creek then altered his direction, while Martin rode on home alone. Jennifer seemed concerned when he came into the house.

"Charlie went to Rock Springs to get a tree for Sales," Martin said.

"Then you must have seen him. Jim, why didn't you say something and save Cal the trouble?"

143

"I didn't see him," Martin said. He was opening his cigar humidor while he spoke, and he had his back to her when he lighted it. "He must have passed me while I was camped for the night. As a matter of fact I didn't get there at all. Changed my mind half way there and turned back." The lie left him feeling a little tight in the chest, and he had to prepare himself before he could turn around and look at her. "Anyway, this is Fred Sales's business, not ours. I bought half of Fred's herd. I offered to ride into town this afternoon and arrange the loan. Likely he'll think about it and come over. He's got to sell or borrow, and he don't have anything to borrow on except the land, and without rain it'll turn to dust."

"And how much does this put us in debt?"

"Nearly three thousand," Martin said. "But I've got four times that in assets, counting the cattle. In another forty days I'm going to ship four hundred head. That'll clear our obligations, and we won't have to borrow a nickel after that." He dropped his cigar in a glass ashtray and came over to where she was sitting. On one knee he assumed a 'proposing' attitude, and she put her arms around him. "Let me make the plans, Jennifer. God knows you'll share everything with me."

"I know, Jim. But don't try to live it all at once. There's time. A whole lifetime before us."

Early Tuesday morning Hansgen's men arrived with the cattle from the Rock Springs rancher, and after the tally, the signing of the papers, Martin invited the three men to stay for dinner. After dinner it wasn't difficult for Martin to persuade them not to go back to Hansgen at all but to stay on. He'd had a new bunkhouse built, and there was a mattress on each bed, and the wages were paid each Friday night instead of once a month. Besides Martin was running the kind of ranch for which a man likes to work where the branding is easy, just a road brand since the owner only buys cattle to fatten them and is not interested in patiently building up a herd of his own, and there are no fences to mend and post holes to dig.

Fred Sales also came over on his way from town. He gave Martin a bill of sale for seven hundred and fifty head, bought for rock bottom prices, and in exchange Martin signed a bank note, which he would take to town at his earliest convenience. Sales's account had been credited with nearly three thousand dollars, and he was in a dour frame of mind about this.

"Three dollars a head for good cattle," he said. "God damn it, you'll sell them in ninety days for twenty dollars a head!"

"Maybe more if the market rises," Martin said. "Sales, you want 'em back? It ain't all profit, you know. They're nothin' but skin and bones. It's my grass and water that'll fatten 'em, and good store-bought feed."

"The water and grass is free," Sales said.

"You fool, Fred, nothing is free!" The man's attitude angered Jim Martin. "You get your tree yet?"

"No, the son of a bitch hasn't come back yet. But you give me time and give me rain and I'll. . . ."

"Is that all you can say . . . 'give me'?"

Sales reared back a little. "By God, now you wait a minute! You got no call to talk to me like that, after all I've done for you. By Jesus, it was my water that made your damned tree grow, so by rights the water you got is as much mine as it is yours. Now you put that in

145

your nose and lump it."

"If that's the way you feel, Fred, I'll give you your water back, just the way I got it, two barrels a week. I'll have one of the men hitch up the wagon, and every week he'll pour two barrels back into your creek. That's fair enough, ain't it?"

Sales was angered to the point of speechlessness. He stared, ground his teeth together, then stabbed his horse with his spurs and rode furiously out of the yard. When Jennifer came to the edge of the porch, Jim Martin was still smiling and looking at the plume of dust Sales raised.

"I don't think you were very fair," she said.

"With Sales," he said, "I can't afford to be. He's staying awake nights figurin' out ways to take this away from me. And he knows I know it."

"Jim, that isn't true! You and Fred have been friends for years." She brushed a strand of hair from her face. "Jim, it isn't like you to think this way."

"Maybe, but it's the way I've got to think."

He took Sales's signed bill of sale into the house, put it with his other documents in a locked tin box, then went into the living room to play a game of checkers with his son. They played until after nine, and Martin took care that he did not win too many pieces. He wanted the boy to learn the feeling of superiority and to know the joy of besting someone, even if it was for fun. The spirit of winning had to be bred into most men. A few — and Martin considered himself one of those — had a natural flair for it.

In the great distance a dull rumble of thunder sounded, and the boy and Martin deserted the game to go outside and look at the night sky. There was a moon,

146

and they could see it now and then through rapidly drifting clouds. The wind was growing stronger now, brushing the grass over.

Martin said: "The first good rain of the year. Hope it don't blow itself out before it gets here."

"Was that thunder I heard?" Jennifer said, coming to the porch. "By golly, it was thunder. Jim, it's going to rain."

"Appears like it," he said, again scanning the sky. "Well, the others can use it." He stepped around the corner of the house and looked north toward the mountains where ragged streaks of lightning darted earthward. "It's raining there. Well, this ought to help the creek. Probably have three feet of water in it by morning."

"It's a blessing for Sales," she said. "The well isn't so important now."

"If you mean the creek will take the place of it, you're wrong." Martin put a match to a cigar. "And Sales has too much money into the well now. He's got to go through with it or fail."

The rain came, gently at first then a little harder, but it never approached the intensity of that earlier rain on Martin's place. This was a good, steady downpour that would last most of the night, and it was covering a wide swath of prairie, starting in the mountains above Rock Springs and carrying on south for miles.

It was a good sound on the roof, and Martin went through the house to see if the new roof leaked. He was pleased to find that it did not. The boy went to bed, and Martin sat out on the porch, his feet cocked on the railing, watching the rain fall. He liked the flavor of it in the air, yet the acute pleasure of it was gone, for he

147

had the sure knowledge that it need never rain for him again. Let it rain for others, and if some fell on his land, all right, but he did not need it with the tree and the well.

A rider came out of the gloom and headed for the porch. Martin watched Cal McKitrich dismount and hurry under the roof. His clothes were saturated for he had no protection. The man who carried a raincape tied behind his saddle in this country was either a fool or an optimist.

"Go in the house. My clothes ought to fit you. The bedroom on the right, just down the hall."

"Obliged," McKitrich said and went on in. Martin heard him speak to Jennifer, then later the marshal came out, wearing one of Jim Martin's suits.

"You ought to get you something like that, Cal. You look fine."

"This suit is worth a month's salary," McKitrich said. "I feel honored just wearing it." He sat down beside Martin. "Charlie Goddard came back tonight. The stage driver brought him in. He's dead. Been dead for some time from the looks of him."

"That's too bad," Martin said softly. "Fred will be broken hearted." He looked at McKitrich. "You told him yet?"

"No. I intended to, but the rain caught me, and I headed here. Jim, Charlie was shot with Fred Sales's gun. I can't rightly figure out how it looks, but I sure want to know where Fred was around the time Charlie was killed." He took out his tobacco, found it soggy, then accepted one of Martin's cigars and a light. "Could be suicide. Charlie was shot from point blank range."

"Maybe Sales can throw some light on it," Martin said.

"You told Charlie's wife yet?" McKitrich nodded. "Jennifer might want to go over tomorrow. She never had much to do with Charlie's wife, but at a time like this women don't think of that. Seems like the land and everything gangs up on 'em, and trouble makes 'em stick together." He took a final puff on his cigar then shied it into the yard. "As a passing thought . . . and I guess it's crossed your mind . . . you've got to figure, too, that Charlie could have been shot by someone. It'd have to be someone he knew real well. Someone he'd let get close enough to shoot point blank. And if he was shot with Fred's gun, it'd have to be someone sort of special, like the fella who owned the gun." He saw McKitrich stare, and Martin shrugged. "I'm just supposin', Cal. If I gave you a gun, would you hand it back to anyone but me, the fella who owned it?"

"You're puttin' poison in my mind, Jim. I've been trying to keep from thinkin' things like that."

"Whoa, now! I'm not accusin' Fred Sales of a damned thing. I'm just tossin' around a few possibilities. Now, I've heard Fred talk against Charlie. He never liked what Charlie did to my boy's dog, and he didn't want anything to do with him. So it does seem a little peculiar for Fred to suddenly want Charlie to do something for him. Or for that matter for Charlie to do it."

"Damn you, Jim, it's hard for me to suspect Fred Sales."

" 'Course it is. But you can suspect me. I was on the Rock Springs Road last week. Never got there, though. Camped out the night on the prairie then came back to town. You talked to me in the hotel dining room."

McKitrich spoke softly. "Jim, I never knew this."

"Well, there wasn't much sense in telling everyone I'd

149

started to do something then changed my mind. But now, since Charlie's been found, I thought you ought to know. Hell, I fought with Charlie in public. The whole damned town saw it. And I made up with him later, right out on the main street. Hansgen saw me. I guess he heard, too. Charlie and I buried the hatchet."

"Jim, are you trying to make a case against yourself?"

"Just telling you the facts, Cal. A law officer ought to have 'em."

"I'll accept that," McKitrich said. "Still, I've been wonderin' why Charlie would commit suicide on a lonely stretch of road where he wouldn't be found for days. The animals and buzzards picked him pretty bad. He'll go to his grave in a sealed coffin." He slapped the arms of his chair. "Well, I guess I'd better go over to Fred Sales's place. Will this suit shrink?"

"Never knew one that wouldn't," Martin said, rising. "But I've got an old poncho you can use." He went into the house to get it, returning a moment later. While McKitrich slipped into it, Martin said: "Cal, I wouldn't arrest Fred if I was you."

"Didn't intend to. Not on evidence as thin as speculation."

He stepped off the porch and mounted his horse. Martin watched the drizzling night swallow him, then went into the house to tell his wife what had happened.

She took it pretty much as he expected her to take bad news, stoically, without tears, for women accepted this sort of thing as a part of living. Martin sat down and began to read some old newspapers while Jennifer went into the bedroom. He supposed that he ought to go over to Goddard's place with her in the morning. Likely there wasn't much money in the house, and

Martin could help Bess and the boy, until they decided what to do. There wouldn't be much to decide really. With Charlie gone the place would go to pot. Probably a sheriff's sale, and Martin wondered how much he would have to pay for it.

Of course, Fred Sales would want it, but the man was a little strapped for cash right now, and it would be late spring before he could market his beef and show a good profit. The rain would bring his grass up, but he had less than a thousand head left, which was not enough if he wanted to buy up Goddard's place.

The regret that Martin had entertained over Goddard's death dimmed a little, and he considered his position with another six thousand acres. Be some time before he could develop it properly, but he could afford to wait while other men could not.

Martin knew that the rain would change Fred Sales's outlook, give him a sense of security that had been missing of late. The rain would make the grass shoot up and put tallow on his steers, and Fred would strut around like the cock on the walk for a while, but Martin was sure that wouldn't last either. He'd go on pushing the well without the tree, and he'd get another dry hole, and the thin bones in his back would break when he added up how much it had cost him. That would be the time to step in and buy him out, Martin decided, or buy him so short he'd spend the rest of his life being a little man and trying to remember what it was like to have been a big one. That would come in the spring or mid-summer, when the hot dry winds blew across the land, withering the grass, shrinking the creek to a trickle. Plenty of time. First Goddard's place, then Fred Sales's. On this thought Martin blew

151

out the lamps and went to bed.

He expected Jennifer to be asleep, but she was not. The lamp at her bedside was turned low. As he undressed, she said: "Poor Bess. And the boy, Jim. What will happen to the boy now?"

"I don't know. What would have happened to him if Charlie had gone on living?"

"But he changed. He swore off drink. That was something, wasn't it?"

His shoulders rose and fell, and he reached for his nightshirt. "I can't worry about the Charlie Goddards in this world, Jennifer. Or the things they leave behind them."

"I was thinking," she said, "perhaps Bess and the boy could stay with us a while, until things get settled in her mind. Would it be all right?"

He looked at her for a long moment, then said: "Strange that you should want another woman in your house, especially one you've never been friends with." He sat down on the edge of the bed and took off his socks. "I'd give it some serious thought."

"You don't want her here, then?"

"Frankly, no," he said. "And it isn't because I'm a mean man, Jennifer. It's a feeling I've got on such a thing. She'll have to do for herself. If it's a hundred dollars she needs. . . ."

"I understand," she said. "Come to bed."

"Thought you wanted to talk?"

She moved over and turned so that she faced him. "All right. The rain sounds good on the roof. It's the first time I ever slept under a roof that didn't leak. No, there was another time. In Dallas, right after we were married." She raised herself so he could slip his arm under her, then she lay close to him, her arm across his chest. "Those were dark days, weren't they, Jim? Or they seemed dark at the time. Now, I can hardly remember them, except that you'd come back for me when everyone said you wouldn't. And the boy had a name."

"Someday," he said solemnly, "I'm going to give you enough of everything so that you'll forget that, and how we started with only three hundred dollars to our name, and with an honor we had barely saved. But the boy must never know, you understand? I don't care what he thinks, or what lies he has to be told, but he's never to know how close he came to being without a father." He sighed and put a forearm over his head. "Yes, they were dark days, Jennifer. But you'll forget them. I'll see to that. I'll live to see you riding in the back of a carriage, and you'll be a grand lady in a flowin' white dress, and a servant'll be holdin' a parasol so the sun won't touch your skin. I'll live to see that, Jennifer, and then I'll be willing to die happy because I'll have given you the best."

She smiled and pressed her lips lightly against his. "If that's what you want, Jim, then that's the way it'll be."

# Chapter Fifteen

The storm died in the night, and the rain stopped. In the morning the sun came out, hot and humid, and steam rose from the ground like thick wood smoke. After breakfast Tad hitched up the buggy and drove his mother to see Bess Goddard while Jim Martin took the saddle horse to town. He supposed he should have stopped and paid his respects, but he thought it better to wait with that, to give Bess Goddard a chance to stop crying, if she cried at all.

After stabling his horse, he went to see Cal McKitrich in his small office. McKitrich had his feet on the desk, his hands behind his head, and his eyes closed. Cigarette smoke hung in layers in the closed room and, when Martin opened the door, it was fanned into brief motion.

McKitrich opened his eyes to see who it was then motioned for Martin to sit down. "Jim, do you think Charlie committed suicide?"

Martin hesitated, wondering what McKitrich was getting at. "I don't know what to say. My opinion wouldn't be worth much, Cal."

"It's hard for me to think of Charlie as a man who'd take his own life," McKitrich said flatly. "Now, you take the man, the kind of man he was. Charlie was always a mean bastard, and I guess, if he was pinned down, you'd find him a little cowardly, but he loved his whiskey and some fun with a common woman. Life was just too damned enjoyable for Charlie ever to destroy it."

Mulling this over in the slow deliberate way he had, Martin said: "Charlie's been ostracized lately. A man gets to feeling pretty low about a thing like that." He shook his head slowly. "Cal, I just don't know."

"I don't think Charlie really gave a damn," McKitrich said. "Hell, he's been kicked out of Herb Manners's place before, and half the people in Morgan Tanks are down on him. His kid's never known what it was to be accepted or to have a father he could look up to. And his wife?" He blew out a breath and slapped his desk. "No, I don't think Charlie gave much of a damn what people thought. And I don't think he shot himself." He took out his sack tobacco and rolled a cigarette. "Still, I don't think I'll ever be able to prove a case of homicide or murder against any man. There's nothing to go on except Fred Sales's gun. And that's too thin, Jim."

"Say, that brings to my mind something Sales once said to me at the creek," Martin said, sitting upright in his chair. "He was givin' me hell for not runnin' out and blowin' Charlie's head off after he killed my boy's dog. Sales said that if he had anything against a man, he'd take care of it."

McKitrich's eyes pulled into fleshy slits. "That's real interesting, Jim. Is that all?"

"By Golly," Martin said, as though he just remembered, "it ain't all! Let me tell you the straight of it now. I brought Fred's horse back, and on the way in I saw Charlie's tracks in Sales's yard. When I got there, Sales was in the house, but I saw him cross from the barn. Charlie had been alone in the house with Edith Sales. Didn't think anything of it until just now. Anyway, Fred let me keep the horse a while longer, but he followed me to the creek, and there's where he said what he did."

McKitrich drummed his fingers on his desk. "God damn it, Jim, every time you open your mouth, you make a case against Fred Sales."

"Hell, I don't mean to." Martin wiped a hand across his face. "All I told you was what I know, what I'd swear to under oath." He started to get up. "Sorry I mentioned it."

"All right, sit down." McKitrich took a long pull on his cigarette. "I hate suspicions, Jim. Give me a case every time but no suspicions. And now that's all I've got. Sales called Charlie over to his place. A couple of Fred's hands saw him there, saw him leave, too. Charlie could have had Fred's gun. He had one when he came into town. I saw it myself. And there could have been something between Sales's wife and Charlie, something Fred didn't like at all. But how am I going to prove anything, Jim?"

"I don't think you can," Martin said, rising. "Best put it down as suicide, Cal."

"No, I can't do that. It'll be death by person or persons unknown."

Martin frowned. "That's leaving the door open for a lot of loose talk."

"Yes, but that's the way it'll have to be," McKitrich said. "Did you want to see me about something, Jim?"

"I guess not. Just wondered what funeral arrangements had been made for Charlie."

McKitrich shrugged. "He'll get buried, and the preacher will try to think of something kind to say. I don't guess there'll be many people there."

"The town ought to turn out," Martin said, "for his wife's sake."

He left McKitrich's office and walked down the street, stopping in Herb Manners's place first. Martin pondered the things he had said, the things he was doing to himself and to Fred Sales, and reasoned that there was no real wrong in it. Charlie's death had been an accident, brought on by the very unpredictable nature of the man. Nothing was to be gained by confessing his hand in it. As for implicating Fred Sales, the man had implicated himself by his own greed, and if the talk hurt him a little, then that was the price a man had to pay for being envious of what his neighbor had.

Martin felt sorry for Charlie Goddard's wife and boy and wanted to do something for them, something that wouldn't really involve him personally. He figured that a good funeral would be the best thing. When he spoke of this to Herb Manners, the saloonkeeper reared back as though a horse had walked on his toe, and Martin had some persuading to do, even a little threatening, before Manners came around and promised to throw his influence Martin's way. There had been times in Martin's life when he'd leaned on men but always with the promise of physical violence, and he felt a little strange, using now his economic influence on Herb Manners. Manners didn't like it, but he didn't blame Martin either, because money men always use their money that way and people expected it of them.

After spending most of the day in Morgan Tanks, Martin went home, feeling sure that a good share of the people would be at Charlie's funeral. It was to be held on Saturday at two o'clock. He was a little surprised at his success. He was not quite used to the power of money, but he was becoming accustomed to it. Manners didn't need Martin to remind him that, when he came in, he stood two rounds of drinks and that usually ate up a ten-dollar gold piece; Manners could add, and he knew a good thing when he saw one. The merchants wanted Martin's business; they all knew he'd be carrying a much bigger payroll soon, and the banker could not afford now to offend his potentially largest depositor. So Martin went home knowing that the town would pay their last respects to Charlie Goddard whether they had any respect or not.

Martin rather dreaded the necessity to stop off at Goddard's place and pick up his wife, yet he forced himself to do this because it had to be done. He wanted to talk to Bess Goddard about buying the place, lock, stock and barrel, and now was the time to do it.

When he dismounted near the porch, he saw the wreath on the door and thought that this was probably something Bess Goddard had kept in a chest for such occasions. She was a proper woman and would have a wreath in case somebody died.

Martin didn't see the two boys. He supposed they were playing somewhere, for children recover quickly from the sadness of a death in the family. He knocked, and Jennifer came to the door. Martin took off his hat and stepped inside.

Immediately he was struck by the poverty, forgetting that only a few months before he would have considered Charlie Goddard lucky to have so much. Tad was sitting in a chair, very quiet, and Pete Goddard was on the horsehair sofa with his mother. He raised his head quickly and stared at Martin with a raw hate.

"You killed my pa," Pete Goddard said, tears springing to his eyes. "I asked you not to, but you done it anyway."

That the boy could so accurately assay the truth shook Jim Martin unbelievably, but before he could say anything, or even compose himself, the boy's mother flipped out her hand and slapped him heavily across the mouth. This shocked Martin as much as the boy's accusation.

"You ungrateful whelp!" Bess Goddard snapped. "Mister Martin's taken his time to come here, and you got to say a thing like that. You ought to be ashamed!"

The boy cried and nursed his bleeding lips, and Jennifer studied her folded hands, biting her lips to remain silent. Martin was just beginning to understand now, and he wasn't sure whether he liked it or not. His son sat in the chair with his thirty-dollar boots, and Jennifer had one of her St. Louis dresses on, and Martin had ridden up on a three-hundred-dollar saddle horse. Bess Goddard wasn't genuinely grieving. She was entertaining her peers and, if her attitude was patronizing, she had to be forgiven for it.

"I'm sure sorry for what he said, Mister Martin. God knows where he gets his wicked notions. If I've said it to him once, I've said it a thousand times . . . you're getting more like your pa every day, God rest his soul." She took a handkerchief and dabbed at her eyes. "It sure was kind of your missus to come over and set with me and the boy. The house is lonely without Charlie. He could be a joy, you know."

Martin tipped his head forward and stared at the knots in the bare floor. He didn't trust himself to look at her while she lied. He supposed this was the one time in her life when she could put on the airs and not have to apologize for it afterward. She could now tell all the little lies about Charlie, and no one would hold it against her.

"The funeral's at two on Saturday," he said. "I've taken care of the details."

"My," she said, "wasn't that thoughtful." She took the boy by the arm and shook him severely. "Now, ain't you ashamed of what you said?" She looked at Martin and gave him a wistful smile, as though she had to work hard to bring it through the curtain of her grief. "Your wife's been such a comfort, Mister Martin. I don't rightly know how to thank you."

"Ah . . . how are you fixed for money?"

"Well, you know how Charlie drank." She glanced at him guardedly. "We don't have much, Mister Martin. Not much at all."

"It's a poor time to talk about it," Martin said, "but you ought to think about what you're going to do. If you're going to work the place, you'll need help, and that takes money. If you're going to sell, I will make you a fair offer."

She shook her head. "I can't see stayin' on. Without my dear Charlie it'd be too much."

"Then we'll talk about it in a few days," Martin said. A glance at his wife was enough to indicate his readiness to leave and her relief at going. They said good bye and went outside. Martin tied his horse behind the buggy and drove toward his place, Tad riding in back, singing and throwing rocks into the drying mud alongside the road.

"It's a shame," Jennifer said, "that she can't say what she feels, that she's glad to get rid of him." She glanced at him and smiled thinly. "God, I thought she'd entertain me to death, Jim. You felt it, too?" She fell silent a moment. "I was proud of you, the way you held yourself when the boy . . . she shouldn't have slapped him. It's terrible to see someone curry for favor. Somehow it insults me, Jim. Probably because many times I've felt like doing it."

"You'll never have to do that," Martin said.

"Yes, I know. Weren't you a little hasty, offering to buy Charlie's place? I mean, she needs some time . . . ?"

"She doesn't need any time," Martin said softly. "Not

160

that woman. She's already made up her mind how much she wants for it." He slapped the horses with the reins, urging them on to a brisker pace.

The sky turned muddy around noon on Saturday, and it began to sprinkle when they gathered at the cemetery to hear the preacher speak for the last time about Charlie Goddard. Martin was surprised at the crowd, and the sincerity of emotion displayed. The men stood solemnly about, acting as though they were burying a dear lodge brother, and the women seemed mournful. Bess Goddard cried and carried on, and the boy, who genuinely missed his father, was unable to cry at all.

After the funeral the men went to Manners's Saloon and bellied up to the bar while the ladies retired to the parsonage for coffee and cake. Martin joined the men in the saloon, not because he wanted to, but because he felt that he had to. He took a place between Cal McKitrich and the banker. Fred Sales stood farther down the bar, morosely staring into his whiskey.

"It was a damned good funeral," the banker said. "Charlie would have liked it." He looked at Martin and laughed. "Now that it's over, I'm glad I didn't miss it."

Martin wiggled his finger at Herb Manners, and everyone had another round. Then Sales slowly turned so that he faced Martin. He had to look past several men to see him. "There's gossip going around about me, and you started it, Jim."

Martin thought carefully before speaking. "Gossip implies that conclusions have been drawn. I never drew any conclusions, Fred."

Carefully, sliding past the other men at the bar, Sales came up and wedged himself between Martin and the

161

banker. "I don't care what you call it, to me it's a low thing to do to a friend."

"Now, just hold on," Martin said. "The day I came to your place to bring your horse back, Charlie was in your house, wasn't he?"

"By God, you watch yourself!" Sales shouted.

Martin held up his hand. "I didn't say anything was wrong, Fred. I just said he was in your house, talkin' to your wife. Now ain't that so?"

"Well, yes," Sales admitted.

"And at the creek, didn't you tell me that if you had anything against a man, you'd do something about it?"

"Jesus Christ, I had nothing against Charlie! What a thing to accuse a man of!"

"Didn't accuse you. Did you say it or not?"

"Well, I did say it," Sales said. "But hell, I was only making a figure of speech." He wiped a hand across his mouth and lifted his whiskey glass. "I didn't do Charlie in and don't make out I did."

"You sent for him, had him come to your place. You gave him your pistol. Suppose you tell us what was it you wanted Charlie to do for you."

Sales stared at him. "God damn it, you know what I wanted."

"Sure, but I guess these folks don't know."

McKitrich spoke up. "Better say, Fred."

Sales looked around for a moment, then laughed. "Hell, it'll sound funny now."

"Then we'll laugh," McKitrich said softly. "What was it, Fred?"

"Well, I wanted Charlie to get me one of them trees like Martin has. Christ, a man can plant a tree, can't he?" He closed his mouth with a snap and, watching

162

him, Martin knew that Fred Sales had been boxed neatly. The man would sound ridiculous if he told everyone that he believed a tree could bring him water, and Sales was too sensitive to endure laughter. He would let them think what they wanted rather than make himself ridiculous before them.

"To hell with all of you," Sales snapped. "Think what you goddamned please. I didn't shoot Charlie, and that's all there is to it." He stomped out of the place, and a moment later they heard his buggy go down the street.

The banker sighed and said: "Hell, you'd think a man could come up with something better than that. A tree? He must think we're stupid."

# Chapter Sixteen

Twelve days of intermittent rain convinced Fred Sales that further drilling was useless, and he abandoned his second well. The driller's bill was staggering, and Sales had to go to Morgan Tanks and borrow on his place to pay it off. Nagging him now was the sure knowledge that he had gambled and lost, and his reasoning was full of "ifs" which were no comfort at all now. *If* this second well had come in, his selling half his herd to Jim Martin would not have been much of a loss, for he would have been in a position to buy three times what he had sold. But the well was a dry hole. *If* he had stood pat and not sold his cattle to Martin, the rains would have given him enough graze to slide through, not with the profit he liked but through just the same without mortgaging anything.

He was in deep now, too deep. He went to Herb Manners's place for a drink. There was little business, and Sales looked out the front window at the muddy street. He saw Jim Martin come into town and tie up near the bank, and a few minutes later Charlie Goddard's widow drove in, tying her team next to Martin's rig.

Herb Manners came from behind the bar to see what Sales was looking at. "I guess Martin's buying her out," he said dryly. "Well, she couldn't have made it alone anyway." He flipped his towel over his shoulder and fished around for a cigar and a match.

"He don't waste any time, does he?" Sales said grudgingly.

Manners looked at him sharply. "What the hell, you'd

have bought it if you'd had the money, Fred. With this rain that sink Charlie had on his place will fill up. Martin ought to be able to run a hell of a big herd all summer, ship early, and make three times what the place cost him. Then if that sink dries up again like it did this year, he can let the land lay idle for three years and still come out ahead."

"Why don't you shut up?" Sales asked. "I know how to run the cattle business."

"Yeah? You're not doin' so good at it." He turned, went behind the bar, and drew a beer for himself. "Fred, is there any truth in the talk going around? I mean, about Martin's tree."

"*Aghhhh,* it's an old wive's tale. Martin was lucky, that's all."

"Yeah, I guess that's it. Still, my old pappy used to tell me that a man made his own luck." Sales turned his head and looked at him for a long moment as though waiting for him to continue. "Let's stop for a minute and add up the score, Fred. Now, Jim's luck has been all good, so there's no sense in going into that. Let's take Charlie's luck first. It turned bad the night he picked up that stray dog and run into Jim Martin. And it ended on the flats, when he was shot down."

"Folks say I did it," Sales said sadly. "Hell!"

"That's all part of your bad luck," Manners said. "Yours started going bad the same night, when you told Jim he couldn't use any more water from your creek. You got mixed up with Charlie Goddard, opened up avenues of talk, spent too much money on dry holes, sold half your cattle, and now had to go see the banker. Borrowing or mortgaging?"

"Mortgaging," Sales said, deciding there couldn't be

any secret about it. The knowledge would be common by evening.

"Now, what a man ought to decide," Manners said, "is whether all this bad luck is accidental or not." Manners shrugged and finished his beer. "My luck's changed for the better. Same with every man on the street. Martin will be putting on some more men one of these days, and they buy booze and play cards and spend money. You know what I think, Fred? I think there's just so much luck in the world, and it keeps getting shuffled around, you know, a little taken away from one man and given to another."

"Yeah, and some men kind of corner a big hunk of it," Sales said. He dropped a quarter on the bar and indicated that he wanted his glass filled again. "That's an interesting idea, about luck. When someone gains, another loses in direct proportion. Yeah, that's real interesting, because you lump Charlie's luck and mine together and all the bad about equals Martin's good." He smiled. "God damn it, Herb, you're a genuine philosopher."

"Well, I do have a few ideas," Manners admitted. He turned his head as steps crossed the porch, then Jim Martin came in. Martin took off his hat, shook water droplets off it, then laid it on the bar. A sheaf of papers protruded from his inside coat pocket as though they had carelessly been thrust there.

"I'm glad to find you here, Fred," Martin said. "Saves me a trip over to your place."

"So?"

"Whiskey," Martin said without looking at Manners. "Well, with a short herd, you'll be thinning your payroll some. I could use four men."

"That would leave me only two."

"Do you need any more than two?"

"No, I guess not," Sales said softly, "All right, Jim, you win."

Martin frowned. "Win? Win what? Hell, I just wanted to keep those men working." He peered at Sales. "If there's something in your craw, better get it out, Fred."

"Why are you trying to break me?" Sales asked frankly. "Is it because you just can't keep from taking advantage of an easy-going man? Is that it?"

"I'm not trying to break you," Martin said. "I've tried to help you. Hell, when you needed cash, I bought half your herd."

"Yeah and talked me into drilling another dry hole."

"Now, wait a minute! God damn it, you made your own decisions, Fred! Don't push this off on me! Son of a bitch, you make me laugh. You got the best piece of land in forty miles, and you're bellyaching about it. You know what the trouble is with you? You're not man enough to make a go of anything when it's really tough." He banged his fist on the bar. "How long do you think you'd have lasted if you'd had my place, huh? You wouldn't have lasted a damned year because you don't have the guts to stand a little trouble." He reached into his pocket and laid two dollars on the bar. "Here, get drunk and forget it. And don't say I never gave you anything."

Martin turned toward the door, and Fred Sales stared after him, anger a stain on his face. Then he picked up the dollars and threw them, hitting Martin in the back. They bounced off and rolled in the sawdust, and Martin slowly turned about and looked at Sales. "You shouldn't have done that, Fred." He took off his hat and coat and laid them on the bar. Then he walked over to where Sales stood.

"All right," Manners said, "let's not have any god-damned trouble in here!"

"I . . . Herb's right," Sales said quickly. "Jim, I lost my temper."

"And I'm losing mine," Martin said, then he stood there, waiting, and Sales looked quickly to Manners then back to Jim Martin.

"I said I lost my temper, didn't I? What more do you want me to say? All right, all right, I'm sorry. Christ, you want to fight over a thing like this?"

"No, I thought you did," Martin said. He picked up his coat and hat then and went out.

After he had gone, Manners said: "Why the hell didn't you hit him, Fred?"

"I thought you didn't want trouble?" He turned angrily to him. "Good God, doesn't anyone know what the hell they want any more?" He blew out a gusty breath. "Hell, I really didn't want to fight him. He could lick me without even half trying."

"Anybody could," Manners said disgustedly. "You want a bottle or not?"

"No," Sales said. "I don't want to get drunk."

"I guess you don't know what you really want either, do you?"

Sales stared at him a moment, then stomped out. He got his buggy from the stable and started home, traveling at a clip calculated soon to overhaul Jim Martin. A mile from town he saw Martin's rig ahead, partially obscured by the drizzling rain. Sales urged a little more speed out of his team and overtook Martin, who stopped to let him pull alongside.

"I didn't pick up the two dollars," Sales said. "I want you to know that."

"You didn't have to prove to me how proud you are. I already knew that," Martin said.

"What the hell are we fighting about?" Sales asked.

"Because the shoe's on the other foot. Because now I have, and you haven't."

Sales shook his head as though greatly saddened by all this. "We were friends, Jim. Good friends. Now I'm kind of afraid of you. Afraid you'll reach out and just pick me off like I wasn't anything at all. Jim, if you'd just give me some sign that it wasn't so, I'd. . . ."

"You want a guarantee, is that it?"

"Christ, I just want to live in peace with my neighbors!" He wrapped the reins around the whip and leaned toward Martin. "Jim, I'd like one of those trees. Just a shoot to plant and make grow. It'd be a gesture, Jim, a real gesture that a man could understand." He cracked his heavy knuckles. "You got one side of the creek now, as much as I have. We could both be big men, Jim. There's room."

"A tree wouldn't help you," Martin said. "Fred, you don't really believe in my tree, do you?"

"Aw, I don't know. But I'll try anything, Jim. By May I'll be burned out again. This piddlin' rain won't raise the creek high enough to carry me through another scorchin' summer."

"Come to me when you believe in the tree," Martin said. "I'll give you a shoot then."

"How'll you know? How'll *I* know?"

"You'll know," Martin said. "But first you'll know what it is to be poor with no hope of changing it. You'll know what it's like to live on a dry piece of land where every

169

swallow of water's counted, where your cattle grow gaunt and walk off the tallow, hunting grass while they eat to put it on. You'll know when you start grabbing at straws to bring rain, praying for it, trying everything, and having it all fail. When that happens, you're ready to believe, accept something with a blind, unwavering faith. Then you'll get a tree to plant. You'll be ready for it then. But you'll never get that far, Fred. You've got the creek, and it'll always have enough water in it to fill your bucket and run a few head of cattle." He thrust his head from beneath the buggy top and looked at the lead-shaded sky. "We've got rain, Fred. And I guess it'll rain a little every year, enough to keep a man going when he has the creek. You'll never know what it is to have it really tough. A man could say that you were lucky there. Before I got my well, I always thought so. I'd have traded places with you any time."

Fred Sales remained silent for a long moment, then he said: "I guess it's no, huh? You're a strange man, Jim. I never really understood you, I guess. All the time you were shooting off that cannon and flyin' the kite, I'd tell Edith you were a little crazy." He laughed without humor. "I guess you were, Jim. I guess wanting something real bad can make a man that way." He unwrapped the reins from around the whip. "I'll send the hands over to you in the morning." Then he urged his team into motion and drove on down the muddy road, the wheel rims lifting and flinging clots against the body of the buggy.

Martin drove on to his own place, taking his time. He wanted to think, to straighten out in his own mind all the complexities of his motivations. He supposed he was like a beggar who finds himself suddenly rich, overwhelmed by the power of money and awed by the effect it has on lives other than his own. And money brought forth a new set of rules by which a man had to live. Poor, one could be honest, for the poor could not afford anything to hide. But money changed that. He would have gone to Cal McKitrich once, when he had nothing, and told him about the death of Charlie Goddard, and he would have been understood, pardoned for the accident. A man's poor station in life was an excuse for error. Now he couldn't do it without being questioned, doubted, or even blamed for something that was not his fault at all. Water and land and cattle created its own loneliness, its own isolation, and he must endure it. He could be hard now for he had to answer to no man, curry for the favor of no man, but what he would have to learn was how to grant favors to others.

He had not treated Fred Sales fairly, he knew, but was helpless to do anything about it. He wanted to help Sales but did not want to appear weak in doing so. When a man was poor, he was weak, but people tried not to step on him out of kindness. But when a man was somebody and displayed weakness, it was an invitation to attack. And this was something he would guard against.

One of his hands put up his team and buggy, and Martin went into the house. There was a fire in the pot-bellied stove to take the chill off the air, and Jennifer was in the sewing room. She came out when she heard him moving around in the parlor.

Martin went to his desk and took the deed from his pocket and locked it in his tin box. "I gave four thousand for it," he said. "She wanted fifty-three hundred."

"It's a lot of land," she said. "Do we need it, Jim?"

He turned his head and looked at her. "It gives me

access to part of the creek and Goddard's sink. I can run two thousand head in there during the rest of the winter and spring." He sat down in his wing-backed chair. "I've hired four more men. Fred Sales is sending them over in the morning." He reached for her hand and pulled her to the arm of his chair. "I've been thinking. In the spring, I want to build a new house. With what I ship, I ought to have over fifteen thousand dollars clear profit. I'd like a big house, two or three stories, something that would rear up out of the prairie for a man to see when he was ten miles away."

"This house is big enough."

"No, no, you don't understand, Jennifer. It isn't what we *need*. It's what a man ought to have." He laughed and patted her plump hip. "Any coffee in the kitchen?"

"I'll get you a cup," she said, and he followed her, sitting down at the kitchen table. After she poured, she sat down across from him and folded her hands. "Can't we stay the way we are, Jim? Everything has changed so much, I hardly know how to keep up with it."

He laughed. "You'll learn, old girl. You still haven't forgot how to make a good cup of coffee."

"Be serious with me," she said. "Jim, where are we going?"

"You and I?" He shrugged. "In all directions I guess. And it's a good feeling. Real good." He pushed his cup and saucer aside and leaned his elbows on the table. "After this year I guess I'll quit buying stock to fatten and ship. A man ought to breed a herd for himself, carry his stock through the seasons. If I had more water, I could do it." He wiped a hand across his face, and speculation came into his eyes, a dreaminess that left them veiled and dark. "You notice the shoots around

172

the trunk of the tree? Some of them are a foot high. I've been thinking of transplanting some of them over on Goddard's place. They can be tended, then in spring I'll sink another well or two. And I'll get more water. What's to stop me, Jennifer? I've got a young, sturdy tree that gives off shoots. I could plant a dozen trees, sink a dozen wells." He laughed, possessed by the idea. "I could cover this whole prairie with trees if I wanted too, and by each one there would be a windmill pumping water." He reached across the table and pinched her cheek lightly. "Two years from now all you'll see is green grass and the brown backs of my cattle."

# Chapter Seventeen

The rains stopped in late February and carpenters came and began to build Jim Martin's new house, choosing for a site a spot a hundred yards west. Martin meant to tear the old house down. He was growing more dissatisfied with it as each day passed. This was a busy month for he had shipped a tremendous herd and had his trees planted on Goddard's place. These were to be tended, watered constantly by one man who made camp by the sink.

Jim Martin's days were long for he had a hundred details to attend to. With a herd sold, there were others to be bought and fattened for late summer shipment, and with building going on he had little time to enjoy his profits. These just kept growing in the Morgan Tanks bank.

He hired a tutor, who came out from Chicago, and Tad had his schooling as a boy should who someday would control a vast cattle empire. Martin had dreams for him, and there was nothing in his thinking to indicate they would not come true.

It was the middle of May before he got a chance to ride over to Fred Sales's place and be sociable. Martin's house was done, the furniture had come overland, and he was having a house warming. Everyone was invited. He used this as an excuse to visit Sales, and he used his heavy work load as an excuse for not coming over before.

In spite of the mortgage and the short herd, Fred Sales had come through the winter with a profit. "My first year as a sharecropper," Sales said, laughing about it. "A friend of mine south of here has had it tough, so he drove his herd north and fattened them here. We split the profit between us. It was better than him going broke and me coming out just even."

"I always said you're a good business man, Fred." Martin got down from his buggy and brushed dust from his suit. A heavy gold-link chain and a walnut nugget fob swayed with his breathing. And because it was an exact hour, his hunting case watch daintily chimed.

"By God, I've never seen anything like that," Sales said. "You mind if I look at it?"

Martin took the watch from his pocket and handed it to Sales, standing close so the chain would reach. Sales popped the lid and examined the face and the beautiful workmanship.

"Got it from in Saint Louis for five hundred dollars," Martin said. "Made in Germany."

"Yeah, those Germans can sure make trinkets," Sales admitted.

Martin put the watch back in his pocket, a little offended. "It's hardly a trinket, Fred."

"Well, I didn't mean it like it sounded." He took Martin's arm and walked him to the porch. From there they could turn and look across the flats and see Martin's house, a vague, high shape against the hazy horizon.

"Been watching that go up," Sales said. "Quite a show piece."

"God damn it! Everything I own is either a trinket or a show piece to you!"

"Now I didn't. . . ." He wiped his hand across his mouth. "What I say just seems to be the wrong thing, don't it?" He opened the door for Martin, then followed him inside.

175

Edith Sales was in the kitchen, and she came to the living room. She seemed older than Martin remembered her, then he supposed a winter of doing her own washing, ironing, cooking, and cleaning had taken some of the shine off her.

"I came to invite you over for the weekend," Martin said. "We're having our housewarming."

"That was kind of you," Edith said civilly.

"We'll be there," Sales said.

Martin realized that he had stayed long enough and went out to his buggy. Sales went with him and, after Martin drove away, Sales went back in the house.

"I guess I should have said no," Sales said to his wife. "Edith, we could afford a new dress for you."

"No we can't, and you know it," she said without resentment.

Sales studied her with sadness in his eyes. He had worked hard during the winter to save a man's wages, and she had worked hard, reddening her hands, going to bed worn out and getting up at dawn still tired. He had to admit that she didn't complain. She had a hard core of stubbornness in her that kept pushing her.

"I'm sorry," he said simply. "I've let you down, Edith. When you said you'd marry me, I promised you you'd never have to scrub a floor, and I haven't kept that promise." He walked over to a chair and sat down wearily. "I know you've been unhappy, Edith. God, I wish you weren't. And I'd like to change it, but I can't. The way I figure, it'll be three, maybe four years before we're back on our feet. Back to where I can buy you nice things and put a servant in the house. I can't rightly hold you here, Edith. I know you've wanted to leave. You know I haven't much money, but there's enough for a

176

ticket East and a little to tide you over."

"Are you trying to get rid of me, Fred?"

He looked at her. "No. I love you, Edith. Loved you from the first minute I laid eyes on you. No, I want you to stay, but I can't hold you to this kind of a bargain. It'll be watching our pennies, and both working hard to save the wages of another man, and doing without. A pretty woman like you deserves better than that."

She came over and stood before him. "Have I been a help to you, Fred?"

He seemed puzzled. "Help? God, I'd have never made it this winter without you. You know that."

"I wanted to hear you say it," she said. Then she knelt and took his hands. "Fred, I've been no good to you until now, and it's a terrible feeling to have, to know you're useless, kept around because someone wants to look at you. You've never needed me before, Fred. Never once, since we've been married have you really needed me. But you need me now, and for the years ahead you'll need me when you come in so tired you can hardly get your boots off. I'm wanted, Fred. For the first time I'm something, somebody important, and I don't want to lose that feeling."

He looked at her in wonderment, then put his hands on her face, and kissed her. "Been a few years since I've done that." He smiled. "Your lips haven't lost their sweetness, Edith."

"I'm going to be a wife to you, Fred. We're together, and we'll stay that way."

"You ought to have a pretty dress to wear to Martin's," he said.

"I'll wear a potato sack," she said, laughing. Her hands were red and rough, and there were tired lines in her face, yet she seemed more beautiful than when he first met her. The petulance, the dissatisfaction, these things were gone, and she had come to terms with herself. She got to her feet and pulled him with her. "Come on, I'll put on some coffee."

Every lamp in Jim Martin's mansion was lighted, and the people of Morgan Tanks deserted the town and overran his house. Outside, in a huge pit, a calf was undergoing the final stages of roasting, and tables were spread by the porch, heavy with food, while inside in the huge main room a five-piece orchestra played a waltz, and dancers whirled and laughed. Tad and the boys from town raced about, dodging in one room after another and running around the porch that circled the house, yelling, playing games. Jim Martin entertained in the library, a gathering of the town's most important men filling the center of the room where the liquor was being dispensed.

"Most impressive," the banker said. "I'll bet it cost you fifteen thousand dollars, Jim."

"Closer to twenty." He waved a hand at the books on the shelves, walls of books. "Those are expensive. All bound in real leather."

"When are you going to get time to read them?" Herb Manners asked.

Martin laughed. "My boy will read them. It's too late for me."

"Never expected to hear you say that," Cal McKitrich said. He wore a dark suit and a celluloid collar that seemed uncomfortable, for he kept running his finger around it and squirming his neck.

"A man can't have everything," Martin said. "The well

driller is coming back. I'm drilling again, on the old Goddard place."

The banker frowned. "That sounds foolish, Jim. Buy and sell, that's the way to make money in this country. Don't let your dreams of becoming a cattle breeder ruin you."

"They won't," Martin said.

"It sounds funny," Manners said, "you calling it the old Goddard place, like old Charlie was still with us?"

"That was a figure of speech."

"Speaking of Goddard," McKitrich said, "his widow's coming back with the boy."

"The hell!" Manners said. "What for?"

McKitrich said: "I guess she didn't like Saint Louis. I got a letter from her last Thursday. She wanted to know if I could find her a job."

"What could a widow do?" the banker asked.

Manners said: "Work for somebody, I guess."

"I thought of you," McKitrich said, looking at Jim Martin. "With this big house, you could use a servant or two."

"I've got four now." He shook his head. "I don't think my wife would like the idea." Then he saw Fred Sales come into the room and waved him over. "Cal was just telling us that Bess Goddard wants to come back and needs a job. You in the market for a housekeeper?"

Sales laughed and shook his head. "As tight as things are with me, I've been thinking of letting one of my hands go. No, it'll be a few years before I can afford a payroll. I'm going to have to make do with one hand, and Edith is taking care of the house." He looked at the banker and laughed. "You want me to hire Bess Goddard or meet your note?"

"Business first, Fred." He winked and offered Sales a cigar.

"Mmm," Sales said, on the first puff. "By God, after heifer dust, these taste pretty fair." He blew smoke toward the paneled ceiling. "It's pure hell to have a taste for ten-cent cigars when you can only afford Bull Durham. You know what I mean, Jim?"

"Yes, but I was able to forget what Durham tasted like. All I remember is that I never liked it."

"It doesn't hurt a man to indulge himself once in a while," Fred Sales said. He tipped his head back and looked at the high ceiling. "How the hell do you ever clean something like that?"

"That's the housekeeper's problem," Manners said, laughing. "Jim's got his mind on high finance."

"I notice that my money rings pretty in your till," Martin said.

"That was a joke," Manners said. "Excuse me while I get another drink. Your whiskey's better than mine." He edged past the banker and pushed through the crowd around the table.

"Jim, can I talk to your wife about Bess Goddard?" McKitrich asked.

Martin frowned. "You've got a one-track mind."

"Well, I like to get a thing settled."

"All right," Martin said, "but I think I've given you the answer."

He had other guests and duties, and he left them, returning to the main reception room where the ladies were gathered with cake and punch. He found Jennifer talking to Edith Sales. She turned when he came up.

"Enjoying yourselves?"

"Yes," Edith said. "I'd get lost in this house."

"Just yell and someone will find you," Martin said. "You're looking well."

"My hands are red, and my back aches," she said, "but I feel fine. It's good to have the days full. I was just telling your wife that I used to envy her because she had something to do." She looked at Martin and laughed. "Don't you believe it?"

"Well . . . no." He touched Jennifer on the arm. "Could I talk to you a minute?" She excused herself and followed him into another room. He closed the door before speaking. "Cal McKitrich has heard from Bess Goddard. She wants to come back if he can find her a job, and he's going to ask you if we could hire her."

"I think that would be nice," Jennifer said. "Pete and Tad could play together and study together."

He frowned. This was not at all what he had expected from her. "Well, I thought you once said you didn't want her in your house."

"Jim, that was before we built this house. " She studied him briefly. "Don't you want her here?"

"I don't think so," he said. "Hell, when they buried Charlie Goddard, I thought we were finished with him."

"Why, what a thing to say! Jim, he's dead, but his wife needs a job. This hasn't anything to do with Charlie." She patted his arm. "If you're set against it, I'll tell Mister McKitrich no."

"No, no," he said hurriedly. "I guess I'm thinking more about the boy than I am about Bess. You know how he accused me. A man doesn't forget that in a hurry."

"Jim, his father had just been found dead. He's gotten over that by now." She smiled. "Is it all right?"

He thought about it and his reservations, then nodded, because she was a kind, gentle woman, and he didn't want to stand in her way about anything. "Sure. You can tell Cal."

She kissed him. "You're a good man, Jim Martin."

He watched her leave and stood there, stripping the wrapper off a cigar, disturbed slightly or perhaps annoyed more than disturbed. Annoyed at Bess Goddard's pushy way of doing this and annoyed at himself for giving in so easily. Well, he'd give it a try, but if Pete Goddard spouted off just once, they'd pack up and leave. He was firm about that.

The party lasted until very late with many from Morgan Tanks and other outlying ranches staying over. Martin had thirteen bedrooms in his new mansion. His watch said a quarter after four when the place quieted down. Jennifer had already gone to bed, and Martin went outside for a final cigar. He saw someone standing farther down the dark porch and walked over, not recognizing Cal McKitrich until he was next to him.

"Some shindig, huh?" Martin asked.

"I've never seen the beat of it." He took a final drag on his cigarette and shied it onto the lawn. "Thanks, Jim. I knew you'd take her on after you'd thought about it."

"Hmm? Oh, Bess. I guess it'll be all right. How come she wrote to you?"

McKitrich shrugged. "I don't know. Maybe she's not satisfied about Charlie. There's a lot of people in Morgan Tanks who think Fred Sales pulled that trigger."

"Oh, bull!"

"You sound damned sure."

Martin looked sharply at him. "Well, I just know Fred, that's all. And you ought to know him, too."

"Yeah, I ought to, but being a lawman a number of years has taught me that I really don't know anyone."

"What a hell of a philosophy," Martin said and went into the house.

McKitrich waited a few minutes, leaning in a relaxed fashion against a porch pillar. Then he began to whistle softly, gaily, as though he were immensely satisfied with himself.

# Chapter Eighteen

Each day the sun was a glittering glass in the sky, the grass wilted, the ground dried to dust, and the only green thing in forty miles was the tree growing near Jim Martin's house. This early summer heat caused him no concern. The well drillers were on their way, and by late June he would have three more wells pumping cool water.

He was a very busy man with a hundred details to attend to and, like so many men growing fast, he was often hard pressed for ready cash. It seemed that he was always paying out money, buying stock, or building this, or drilling for more water. Still, money was not difficult to raise since he was a man of substance with assets, and on paper he was quite well off.

Martin's dream of owning so much property that he would have difficulty seeing it all was realized and, when he saddled a horse to ride over to the sink on Goddard's old place, he realized that he had not been there since ordering the small trees planted. He felt a touch of guilt about this, remembering how he had tended the first tree, thinking only of it and little else. He had neglected these three new trees but only personally. They had received the best of care and attention. Yet, with the drillers on the way, he felt that he ought to have a look and perhaps pick the sites for the wells.

The thought of more water stirred in him a deep elation. He could pump the sink full and leave it full and turn the land around it into an oasis, into a sea of tall grass, the finest grazing land a man ever saw. The simplicity of it made Jim Martin feel smug. All he had to do was to have one of his hands dig a hole and plant a shoot off his tree, pour a little water on it, then dig another well. He could not imagine the end of the fortune he could amass this way.

Finlay Teeter was the young man who camped by the sink. For a month his duty had been simple yet exacting: to carry buckets of water to the three little trees and nourish their roots. He was by his fire when Martin rode up and dismounted. Teeter grinned and scratched his beard stubble. "Sure gets lonesome out here," he said. "Coffee, Mister Martin?"

"Thank you, no. The driller and crew should be here any day now. Are the trees healthy?"

Teeter cuffed his battered hat to the back of his head and seemed puzzled. "Don't rightly know much about trees, Mister Martin. Up to now I just noticed that they was shady and good for sleepin' under when I got tuckered."

"Never mind," Martin said and turned away from Teeter's camp, walking a few hundred yards to where the first tree had been planted. His eyes looked for leafy greenness, expected it, and he found nothing except a withered stick in the ground, the tiny limbs shriveled and dead. Martin stared in disbelief. The ground was a puddle of mud around the small tree. Teeter had watered it faithfully, yet it had not grown one inch.

Running, he circled the sink to the other two trees. They were the same — dead sticks thrusting up out of the muddy ground. He could not understand this. What had he done wrong? Had he damaged the trees in carrying them here? He didn't think so because he had wrapped the roots and kept the burlap soaked and

185

carried the trees in the buggy so that not one leaf would be crushed.

Martin was convinced that he had done nothing wrong. He would have to search elsewhere for the answer. But where? What could account for this — this betrayal? The tree by his house was healthy and growing at a fantastic rate, and these small shoots were offspring. They should have grown, flourished with the same care.

He sat down to think, to decide what he should do. Try again with new shoots? He decided against that, feeling certain of failure as this planting had failed. Then he considered the driller and crew that were due to arrive any time. Could he risk sinking a well here without a growing tree beside it?

Martin hesitated over this but not for long. He could afford to put down one well just to see what would happen. He could gamble that much. The notion was floating around in the back of his mind that he didn't need the damned trees at all. His disappointment prompted this, and the notion was still there when he mounted his horse and rode on back to the house. He could afford to put down a well anywhere and any time he pleased, and by God he'd get water, or he'd drill to Hades for it! There was an undisputed sense of power in Martin. He felt that nothing could hold him back. He was capable of doing anything and, if he wanted water, he'd dig, and water would be there.

There was no sense in leaving Teeter by the sink so, when Martin got home, he told the foreman to put him to work somewhere else. He left his horse in the barn for one of the hands to unsaddle and, as he walked to the house, a sense of unreality struck him sharply, and he stopped to think about it. Not

186

long ago he had been familiar with every facet of his work, his ranch, but now he knew almost nothing of the details. He concerned himself with only the overall picture, the long-range planning, thinking three years ahead now instead of three days. He knew Tip. They had bellied against the same bar many times. He knew the others, too, but he no longer noticed them or spoke to them. All orders were given through Tip, all knowledge of the work came through Tip. Martin felt like a stranger who had lost touch with himself. There was no place to turn to reëstablish his identity.

Going on into the house, Martin went to the library. Mrs. Goddard came in almost immediately with a tray containing coffee and some cookies. She put this on his desk and waited.

"Thank you," Martin said. "Is Missus Martin at home?"

"Yes, sir. She's in the morning room."

Martin had to think a minute before he figured out which room that was. This was the trouble with a big house, you never knew where anyone was in it. In that respect he disliked his mansion intensely and thought often of the other house, where he could step in the door and hear his wife working, or singing, or call out and have her answer him. Here a man could fire a pistol upstairs and never have it heard in the library.

"Tell her I'm back," Martin said.

"Yes, sir." She turned to the door then stopped. "Mister Martin, it was kind of you to take me and the boy in and. . . ."

"I thought we weren't going to talk about it?" Martin reminded her. "Go on now. I've got work to do." She went out, and he sat down behind his desk, his manner thoughtful. His former reservations about havin  m in his house had all but vanished and the only remaining one was the boy, Pete. Martin could see in his eyes that he had never changed his mind one bit about his father's death, and this troubled Martin because he didn't know what to do about it. Pete got along fine with Tad, but now and then Martin would turn around and find Pete staring at him, and for an hour afterward Martin could still feel the chill of those eyes. Several times he'd started to say something to Jennifer, then thought better of it. A feeling like that was hard to put into words and sound convincing, especially to a woman like Jennifer who couldn't believe there was real evil in anyone.

He spent the rest of the day going over his books, trying to find out how much money he had to spend on his gamble with the well. He had decided to go through with the drilling without the trees. The decision was forced, and he had to keep telling himself that it was the logical thing to do, the realistic thing to do. And he made himself stop wondering why the three little trees had died. It no longer mattered. He no longer needed them and, if the well came in, he would have his proof, proof that he was past the point where he had to call on strange gods for what he wanted. He was a man who desired everything to be of his own making since it gave his accomplishments more importance and value.

Dinner was at seven, but the driller's untimely arrival interrupted it. Martin had one of the hands take the driller and his crew and wagons to the sink. They could make camp there, and he arranged for a chuck wagon to follow them and feed them while they worked. By the time this was taken care of, the dinner was cold, and he had a sandwich in the parlor.

Tad and Pete played on the rug with some kind of a

toy Martin had ordered from Chicago. He watched them, trying to figure out what the game was, then gave it up as not being very important. Jennifer sat across an expanse of expensive rug, sewing on something or other. He no longer paid any attention to what she was making.

"Beef has dropped fifteen cents," he said, and his voice seemed to ring in the silence. Everyone looked at him as though startled.

"I hope it isn't a trend," Jennifer said. "We're over-stocked, aren't we?"

"Not when I get another well in," he said.

"The boys will have to ride out and watch them drill," she said. "It'll give them something to do."

"Don't they have anything to do?" Martin asked. He looked at Tad. "How are you coming with your studies?"

"All right," he said.

"You ought to talk to Mister Barsotti," Jennifer said. "He's been here nearly seven weeks, and you haven't spoken to him." She put her sewing aside. "Jim, it's a very odd feeling to know that Mister Barsotti is living in the south wing of the house and never hear him or see him for days on end."

"That was the point in building the house large, so we could have both privacy and convenience. What are you boys playing?"

"Chess," Tad said.

Martin laughed. "I suppose Mister Barsotti taught you that?" Tad nodded his head. "Well, when I was a boy, I played mumblypeg."

"Poor kids play that," Pete Goddard said. Then he looked at Jim Martin. "You've got lots of money, ain't you, Mister Martin?"

Martin was not sure what he should do, put the boy

in his place or answer him seriously. He said: "If you mean, do I have a lot of cash, then you're wrong. A man invests his money, Pete. I buy skinny cattle, fatten them, and sell them for a profit."

"Mister Barsotti says you're a speculator," Pete said. "Ain't that so, Tad?"

"I didn't hear him say that," Tad Martin said. He glanced at his father, and in the brief meeting of their eyes Martin knew that Barsotti had said that and meant it.

"There's nothing wrong with business speculation," Martin said. He leaned forward and looked at Pete Goddard. "You don't like me, do you?"

"Aw, I guess you're all right. Besides, Ma'd lick me if I said anything."

"I see. Go on with your game, boys."

The front door knocker woke echoes through the house, and Mrs. Goddard hurried down the hall. A moment later Cal McKitrich came in.

"I brought back your suit," he said, indicating a bundle under his arm.

"You could have kept it," Jim Martin said and saw the instant resentment in McKitrich's eyes.

"I wasn't looking for a handout when I borrowed it," he said softly. "Jim, you're getting pretty high with people. It's about time you came down and scuffed a little dust with the rest of us common people." Then he smiled and bowed slightly to Jennifer. "You're looking right handsome, Missus Martin."

"Thank you, Marshal. Won't you sit down?"

He placed his hat on the floor and took a chair across from Jim Martin. Jennifer got up, pulled a sash along the wall, and a moment later Bess Goddard appeared.

"Could you bring us come coffee, Bess?"

"Yes'm."

When she was out of earshot, McKitrich brushed his mustache and said: "Working out all right, Jim?"

"Hmm? Oh, yes. Fine, Cal." He fell silent and moved his hands restlessly. "What brings you out here?"

"Oh, just some talk," McKitrich said. "You know how I am, Jim. I get to thinking about something, and I keep thinking about it."

"Like what?"

McKitrich glanced at the boys. "Ain't it about their bed time?"

He wanted them out of the room and hesitated. Then Martin said: "All right, boys, let's hit the shucks."

They protested and made a fuss about it, but they went, yelling and running down the long hall, dashing up the wide stairs, banging doors. Martin offered McKitrich a cigar and a match. The marshal leaned back in his chair and puffed gently.

"I've got to hand it to you, Jim, your taste for good things is the best." He crossed his legs and smiled. "Don't look so worried. I didn't come here to arrest anyone."

"Then get to the point."

Bess Goddard returned with a tray. There was no more talk until she left the room. McKitrich lifted his cup, tasted it, then set it down to cool a little. "Jim, did you ever go back to Rock Springs and thank that fella who gave you the tree?"

"I thanked him the night I brought it home," Martin said. "Why?"

"Just something I wondered about, that's all." He laughed briefly and drank some of his coffee. "Jim, tell me the truth now. Is there anything to the talk about this tree bringing you water?"

"No," Martin said and felt a ringing in his ears as though some of the passages were clogged up. This was a bold thing for him to say, and he wondered what made him say it. He supposed there was a touch of defiance in his voice, as though he meant to prove to himself that it had all been his imagination and that everything he had was of his own making.

Jennifer stopped sewing and looked at him. "Jim, you know you believed. . . ."

He held up his hand. "Yes, I guess I did. But it was the thinking of a desperate man. You know what I mean, Cal? A man will think strange things when his back's against the wall, and he's about finished." He laughed softly. "I guess there was always water on my place, but I had to be driven to dig for it . . . driven to it and convinced that I wouldn't fail. That's the part you've got to understand, that I couldn't have taken another failure."

"But now you can, huh?"

"Yes, it wouldn't bother me now," Martin said. "I could weather it without bleeding." He picked up his cigar and puffed it back to life. "One of these days I ought to go to Rock Springs and look up that old man. That's a damned nice shade tree, you know. There isn't another like it within fifty miles."

"How come you said that?" McKitrich asked.

Martin took the cigar from his mouth and stared at him a moment. "Why, because it's so. You think I'd say a thing if it wasn't so?"

McKitrich leaned back and studied Martin carefully. "Jim, you told me you camped out on the flats the night

Charlie Goddard was shot. I think you went to Rock Springs."

"What reason would you have to think that way?"

"From what you just said. How did you know the old man's tree had been cut down, Jim?"

Martin saw his error and shrugged and twisted around in his chair. "Why, I guess I heard about it. From someone in town."

"No, you've been too busy with your own affairs to pay any attention to what's going on around you. Sales didn't shoot Charlie. We both know that. What did you shoot him for, Jim?"

Denial was close to the surface of Martin's mind, then he blew out a ragged breath and said: "I met him on the road. He had a gun. Talked big. I knew he was going to shoot me, so I jumped him. We wrestled a little, and the gun went off. I left him there."

"You should have told me before," McKitrich said softly. "But you let people believe Fred Sales did it." He rose and picked up his hat. When he turned to the hall, Martin got up also.

"Are you arresting me, Cal?"

"No," McKitrich said. "I'll leave it to you to straighten out."

"What can I do now!"

"You figure it out," the marshal said and left.

It was in Martin's mind to tell him to stay the night, but he really didn't want McKitrich in the house now. He didn't want anyone around until he had a chance to think this out. He cursed himself for being such a fool, telling McKitrich straight out like that, but he couldn't help himself. The words burst from him as though he no longer had any control over them, and he knew how subtly he must have been fighting this all along. Looking at his wife required genuine effort, but he forced himself to look at her, expecting condemnation in her eyes. But there was only perplexity, concern, bewilderment.

"Jim, why? Just tell me why you lied, kept this to yourself."

He shook his head sadly. "God only knows. I'd like to blame it on my dreams. They were big, Jennifer, and I didn't want anything to stand in the way of them."

"Dreams? I don't understand them any more, Jim. You want the moon and the earth and the sun and you shoot poor Charlie and say not a word about it . . . I don't understand any of this." She pointed to the upstairs of the house. "And Pete, living here with you, eating at your table . . . doesn't it bother your conscience at all, Jim?"

"Yes! yes! yes!" he shouted. Then he calmed himself and rekindled his cigar. "Good God, Jennifer, only poor Jim Martin could have gone to McKitrich with the truth, don't you see that? Poor Jim Martin did things by accident, never deliberate intent. This Jim Martin had to keep silent."

"Who is this Jim Martin?" she asked flatly. "Be truthful now and answer me. Isn't he a little man who barely finished the sixth grade who found water on the plains? Isn't he a man who got his hands on a few dollars that wasn't spoken for and had it make him drunk?"

"No! No, that ain't so!" He whirled to her, glared at her. "By God, all the time I ate dirt and walked around with empty pockets, I was thinking of a time when maybe I wouldn't be hog poor! Some people can live poor, and it doesn't bother them, but it bothered me. I hated to be poor. I hated it so much it was a gnawing in my belly and an ache in the back of my head, and I wanted money

194

more than a woman." He jammed his hands deeply into his pockets and bit into his cigar. "God knows I've changed, Jennifer, and lying to you, to everyone about Charlie wasn't to my liking. But is it something you can't forgive?"

"Do you need my forgiveness, Jim?"

He frowned.

"Do you really need it, Jim? Is it important to you now what I feel or think?"

"That's a foolish question," he said.

"No, it's a very serious one. One of these days you'll ask yourself if you need me any longer. You've already decided that you don't need the tree, or you wouldn't have told it to McKitrich."

"I just didn't want him to laugh, that's all."

"He wouldn't have laughed. He never did when you flew kites and shot gunpowder." She studied him carefully. "Jim, I've never really been sure about the tree, or about some of the other things you've believed. Perhaps the tree did bring water. I don't know. I wouldn't say it did, and I wouldn't say it didn't. I only know that I wouldn't tamper with Providence, Jim. We've had luck in our life, and most of it's been bad. But you've had a streak of good now. Don't waste it, Jim. Don't throw it away."

He laughed at her as though he considered her concern a little foolish. "I'm making my own luck from now on," he said.

"You don't really believe that."

"I proved I could get water," he said. "Do I have to prove that, too?"

"What do you mean?"

"Those trees I had planted by Charlie's sink died. They

were watered, but they just wouldn't take root and grow."

A touch of fright came into her eyes and into her voice. "Jim, what does it mean?"

"Mean?" He shrugged. "I don't know and don't care. I'm drilling anyway, and I'll get water without the damned trees." He sat down by her and took her hand. "Jennifer, trust me. Believe in me. I said once that when a man got his strength, he really didn't need anything else. I feel that way now, strong, sure of myself. When I brought the tree home, I was on my knees, bleeding, ready to roll over and die. But it's all changed now. I'm strong, and there isn't anything I need any more to hold me up. I have my own faith. Can you understand that?"

"Yes," she said. "And I wish I didn't understand it. I wish a wind would come up and blow the house down and that we were back where we started. We knew each other then, Jim."

"We know each other now!"

She shook her head. "No, we don't. If you'd shot Charlie then, I know what you'd have done. You'd have gone to Bess and the boy and cried with them. But you'd never do that now, Jim."

He opened his mouth to deny this, then closed it, and got to his feet. She was right, and he wished she wasn't so right. All right, he'd changed. She'd just have to understand him. Taking out his gold watch, he popped the face lid, glanced at it, and said: "I think I'll go to bed. I want to go out to the sink early and watch them set up the drill rig."

# Chapter Nineteen

When only he possessed truthful knowledge of Charlie Goddard's death, that truth had been vaguely disturbing, and Jim Martin managed to live with it. But now McKitrich knew because he had gone to Rock Springs and had seen the fallen tree, and Jennifer knew, and the truth had become a constant worry. Every time Martin saw Bess Goddard moving about the house, he was troubled more and more, and he could not bear to look at the boy at all. Still nothing changed. Pete and Tad studied together and played together, and their lives went on with unbearable certainty until Martin thought he would explode. He took to staying away more, leaving early in the morning and returning at night when the boys were in bed. He had excuses — the pressure of his work, the new well that was thumping deeper into the ground, and the business of buying and selling cattle which he continued to expand at an alarming rate.

From the surrounding hard-pressed ranchers Martin had bought all there was to be bought, and he began to have cattle shipped in from as far as North Texas and Dakota. He made money selling and spent it buying until his finances were in a continual state of flux, which worried the banker but worried Martin not at all.

He was going to get water from his new well and, when he got it, he would not be overstocked. But right now he was, dangerously so. Beef prices had dropped sharply, which was good for buying but not for selling, and Martin was gambling that they would rise in two or three months. He meant to ship at least forty-five hundred head, and he needed a two hundred and fifty percent profit. The driller was down seventy-five feet and still going deeper, and there was nothing encouraging in the muck he kept bringing up, yet Martin was determined to continue.

He wanted to go over to Sales's place and see how he was coming along. The man was playing it safe, building again very slowly, paying off what he owed, trying to climb out of the hole he had dug for himself, trying to get water. Martin's conscience bothered him where Sales was concerned. Sales was a simple man, susceptible to suggestion, impressed with the success of others and, knowing this, Martin had led him down the garden path to near ruin. Logically, Martin blamed Sales for being his own fool, but morally Martin blamed himself. He wanted to do something for Sales, not to make up for anything but to free his mind from the guilty sense of obligation.

Sales had to have more water. What dribbled through the creek was not enough. Another attempt at well drilling was out of the question, for not only was it expensive but a great gamble. But a dam wouldn't be a gamble, Martin decided. Expensive, yes. Expensive as putting down another well, but it would raise the water level in the creek, fill it to the banks, and insure Sales of year-around water.

After thinking about it, after deciding to go ahead with it, Martin's wife made no comment at all for she understood why he chose to spend three thousand dollars, which he couldn't afford to spend. And, when the citizens of Morgan Tanks heard about it, they said that Jim Martin was a great man, the kind of a man who made a country and that someday they'd erect a statue of him

198

in the park. The banker considered Martin's plan sheer insanity. He would have to borrow the money to get the job done, and he was already in debt, but the banker was actually helpless for he had to loan the money, had to keep Martin going. To cut him off now would be to lose everything he had loaned him.

Martin rode over to Sales's place on a Wednesday afternoon to talk it over. He was a little irritated at Sales's lack of enthusiasm. Sales was impressed by the offer yet suspicious of it, and Martin talked, trying to dispel the suspicion but only succeeding in driving it deeper. When he left, he was a little sorry he had gone to all this trouble for Sales, but he had already hired the men, bought the timber, and turning back now would be foolish. The work was going to start on Monday.

His well was down ninety-seven feet and still there was no sign of sandstone. Martin acknowledged a tinge of worry, but he ordered the driller to continue and drove to the creek in his buggy to see how the crew was coming with the dam. Martin wasn't sure how far south the creek ran or how many other ranches it served, but he was especially careful not to close off the flow of water completely. The workers were sinking the base shoring, building the vertical piling, then laying in the timbers, allowing the water always to flow over. Martin's idea was to build the dam at least twelve feet thick, with a small bridge over the flood gate so that a wagon or horseman could use it to get across. Daily the water backed as the timbers went higher and the filling began.

Daily, also, the driller's steam rig puffed and punched away at the earth and, by the time the dam was backing a good head of water in the creek, the driller had raised the first sign of St. Peter's sandstone, a good indication that he would get water. A tremendous weight seemed to lift from Jim Martin, and he knew then how much subconscious worrying he had done, and how many were his hidden doubts. When Hansgen, the cattle buyer, rode out from town, he found Martin in a generous frame of mind.

Cattle prices had dropped again, and Hansgen was worried about it for Martin was overstocked and, if this well didn't come in, he'd have to sell some skinny beef at two dollars a head less than he had paid for them. This was enough to make any investor toss sleeplessly in his bed. But Martin's confidence was full again, like a bucket unable to hold more. The well was due to come in any day now, and Hansgen went back to town with some of Martin's surety rubbed off on him. Only it was like the shine on cheap brass, quickly tarnishing. Hansgen had only to look around at the sea of sunburned grass to know that Martin had gone too far in his climb and was ready to lose his grip and fall. And there wouldn't be anything to stop that long hard drop to the bottom.

When the dam was finished, a man would have had to swim his horse across the creek to the other side if the causeway hadn't been there. The water was that deep. It was backed up and stretched out nearly twenty yards across, and Sales stood there on his side and looked at it, water such as he had never dreamed of, such as he would never have been able to provide for himself. Always he had been in a position where it took money to make money, and he'd never had enough. Now he would grow, perhaps not as Martin had grown. He had never known the want or felt the nagging needs

Martin had felt, but he could do now in a year that which would have taken five years, and he was grateful beyond words.

He met Martin on the causeway and said: "I can put up a windmill and pump water now." He was too emotionally touched to say more. He merely wrung Martin's hand and rode home.

"I've paid him back," Martin said softly as Sales rode away, and he turned to his own place, feeling just the same as he had felt before the dam was built. Then he knew that he hadn't paid anything. There would only be one way to pay — tell Sales he was sorry, tell him what really happened, so that everyone would know and not think any longer that Sales had killed Charlie Goddard. And Martin knew that he couldn't do that. It wasn't in him to go to Fred Sales with the truth.

Tad brought the news, dashing in with Pete Goddard, riding double. They flung off in the yard and banged into the huge house, running from room to room until they found Martin.

"It's in! It's in! The well's in!"

Then they ran out, leaving Martin with his relief and his silent thanks that his faith had remained unshaken. When he went to the barn for his horse, he felt light, elated, sure now that the power of the tree was a dream, a figment of his desperate imagination. His well was in, clear water, and without a tree. The water was there because he had wanted it to be there, because he needed it there.

Near six hundred feet, the driller said, and Martin would have to pump to get a substantial volume. On the spot Martin contracted to have the windmill erected and the water piped to the sink. In sixty days he'd have an all-year-around lake nearly a hundred feet across and thirty feet deep, enough water to clear his debts, allow him to ship on schedule, and make his tremendous profit. He supposed he ought to let the banker and Hansgen know. They'd be relieved. So, when he went back to the house, he sent a rider into town to tell them.

That evening, for the first time in nearly four weeks, he had dinner with his family, and afterward he went into the parlor with Jennifer. The boys went to the barn where a mare was about to foal. Martin wanted to relax now, but he found it impossible, and he told himself that the strain of the last weeks was the cause of it. He would need a few days to unwind. His wife read a magazine, and Martin walked about the room, touching bric-a-brac and fixtures and pieces of furniture as though he had never seen any of it before.

Finally Jennifer put the magazine aside. "Can't you sit still, Jim?"

He turned around and looked at her, then laughed. "I got my well just like I said I would."

"Yes. It must make you very happy."

He frowned. "Well, you should be happy, too." He came over and flopped in a chair, stretching his legs out in front of him. "It seems to me you don't care much any more, Jennifer. You're just not with me in things any more."

"How can I be? We don't work together now," she said. "And you've run so far ahead so fast, I can't catch you."

"What do you want to do, ride around with me?" He shook his head. "I don't understand your thinking on this, Jennifer."

"Are you sure it's my thinking and not yours? Jim,

it didn't help a bit to build the dam for Sales, did it? It didn't tell him the truth or make it any easier for you."

"It's too late now," Martin said. "The time to have told him was the next day. He'll never understand why I waited."

"Does he have to understand? Does he have to forgive you for it?" She compressed her lips slightly. "Do you think Pete will forgive you?"

"No, I guess not, but he'd believe me. He'd believe it was an accident."

"And that isn't good enough, is it? He has to forgive you."

"Good God, I'm human! I want to be liked!" He calmed himself. "And I want my wife to believe in me, Jennifer. I want my wife to love me."

"Jim, I do love you. If I didn't, I wouldn't care what you thought or felt, or what you did. You're not honest with yourself any more, and it hurts to see that. And you're not honest with other people, either. When we didn't have anything, you gave everyone honesty, which is a valuable thing. But now you have money, and you give them that instead. You gave the dam to Sales instead of the truth. And you've given Pete a home and clothes and an education instead of the truth. That hurts me to see, Jim. If this is what I have to pay to have luxury, then I want to be poor again." She regarded him steadily. "I want to go back before you give me money instead of the truth."

He was shocked. "That is a hard thing to hear from you."

"It's the truth," she said simply. "Well, you've got water again and a feeling that you're right. What little I can say won't change anything or the way you believe. Jim, never forget where you got all this. God gave it to you to use. Use it wisely."

"What makes you think I'm not?" He slapped his hands together half angrily. "Look what I've built. It's a thing to be proud of. Hell, have you forgotten the cattlemen in Texas, owning a half million acres, living like kings? Did either of us ever look down on them?" He laughed. "Hell, we dreamed of being like them. Don't you remember how we talked and envied the way they lived? You say God gave me all this? What about the years I broke my back and went without? Doesn't that count for anything, Jennifer?"

"Yes, I guess it does, but only toward making you worthy. Jim, don't forget how desperate you were for water. Don't forget how you planted the tree and nursed it."

He looked oddly at her, puzzled, confused. "I thought you never believed in the tree. Now you talk like you do."

"It isn't that I believe or disbelieve," she said. "But God moves in mysterious ways, Jim. Don't offend Him."

"This is nonsense," he said. "I don't need the tree. Look at what happened at Charlie's sink. The trees died, but I got a well anyway. That proves to me that I just wanted hard enough to believe some old man who was touched in the head. I guess I'll have to prove it to you, too."

His talk frightened her. "Jim, don't be a fool now!"

"I'm not," he said. "There's some things a man's just got to know, whether he's his own man or God's tool." He got up and went out, slamming the door, and after a moment's hesitation she followed him.

Martin was talking to Tip near the porch. "Fetch me a crosscut saw, some wedges, a maul, and a sharp axe."

"Yes, sir," Tip said and trotted across the dark yard to the tool shed.

Jennifer grabbed Martin's arm. "What are you going to do?"

"Cut down that damned tree," Martin snapped. "And, after it's down, you'll see that the water still comes from my well." He wiped a hand across his face. "Old man Patchin's well went dry when I cut down his tree, but it won't go dry for me. I got water without any more trees, didn't I? I'll keep my water now without it. Besides, the damned thing drinks an intolerable amount. It's about time I'm gettin' shed of it."

"You fool! You're not God!" She took him by the arms and tried to shake him, but he pushed her away.

"I ain't trying to be," Martin said. "I've just got to know if I'm running my own affairs or not." He pointed to the tree. "You think I want to live the rest of my life out, wonderin' if I dare cut a branch off it or not?" He turned her and gave her a shove. "Go on back in the house. I made it grow, and I'll kill it."

She retreated a step and stood there, stubbornly refusing to go further. Tip returned with the tools, and Martin took off his coat and vest and threw them on the ground. Seizing the axe, he sank a deep cut into the tree, then worked with a fevered frenzy, making his undercut deep and wide, flinging chips with his axe, shaking his head to clear his eyes of sweat. The hands came from the bunkhouse and watched, and the boys left the barn. Tad stood by his mother as though to gain some protection from the terrible thing that was bound to happen when the tree toppled.

He chopped for an hour then flung the axe aside and picked up the saw, making his fall cut on the other side and higher than the notch cut. When the blade was deep and threatening to pinch, Martin drove in his wedges, and the tree groaned and stirred, and the sawing went on. When it began to go, the movement was slow, reluctant, then it fell with a rush and a crackling and thundered when it hit the ground, bouncing and spraying leaves and twigs.

Martin had jumped clear of the thrashing trunk, and he looked at the pipe running from the well. Water still trickled undiminished from it, and he motioned toward the scattered tools. "Put them away," he said, and a man bent to pick them up.

He took off his sweat-soaked shirt and rolled it into a ball before throwing it on the ground. Then he put on his vest and held his coat over his arm, still watching the water cascade from the pipe.

"Now do you see?" He looked at his wife. "Now do you believe what I say?"

"I've never doubted what you said," she replied softly. "But I'm sorry you ever found this out, Jim. Before you knew, there was still some caution in you. Now there's none." She took Tad by the arm and turned, and they went into the house while he stood there and watched the water run strongly and purely from the pipe.

# Chapter Twenty

If Jim Martin had any regrets about cutting the tree down, it was only that he missed the magnificent shade it had given. There was no slackening in the strength of his well, and he had the pipe taken down that had once run to the tree to keep it watered. His windmill at the sink was up and pumping water through a four-inch pipe, and daily he could see the water rising. He selected an arbitrary level and then put his crew to work digging trenches out from the sink like giant spokes of a wheel and, from these, additional fingers, so the water would overflow and spread and irrigate a vast section of land, making the grass thick and green and his cattle very fat.

Much of his time now was spent in town, watching the market. The price of beef was very low, but it seemed to have stabilized considerably, and Martin held onto the hope that it would soon rise. Hansgen, who was less of an optimist, wasn't so sure. He kept advising Martin to sell, making a lesser profit but to clear himself of debt while he could. Martin only agreed to think it over.

A good deal of time was spent in Kinred's bank for the banker was in some ways Martin's partner. The investment was that large. Kinred was a man dedicated to a conservative course through life, and Martin worried him, for Martin believed that he couldn't help but make money. Taking rooms in the hotel, Martin stayed in town for nearly a week, and he spent his evenings in Herb Manners's place, buying drinks, talking, giving advice, and spreading his optimism about like gifts. He saw McKitrich often, but they really had nothing to talk about. Then Fred Sales came in to do his shopping, and he saw Martin in the saloon.

"I've got to buy you a drink," Sales said, urging Martin to belly up against the bar. "Two of your best whiskey, Herb." He turned to Martin and put his arm around his shoulders. "You know, we're gettin' along across the creek, Jim. Yes sir, by George, we're goin' to make it. Why, likely by winter I'll put on another hand, if the prices don't fall out on beef."

"How many head are you running?"

"With the calves dropped, I'd say nearly eight hundred," Sales said. "And the pretty part of it, now that I'll have a full creek all summer long, is I won't have to sell unless the price suits me. I can get through thanks to you, Jim."

Manners put the drinks on the bar, and they lifted them, then set the glasses back empty. "A man just can't get along without water," Herb Manners said. He looked at Jim Martin and smiled. "I guess I've got a little piece of your place, come to think of it."

"How's that?" Martin asked.

"Well, I've got money in the bank. About fourteen hundred dollars give or take a little. Kinred only had seven thousand when he started the bank, and since you've borrowed almost fifteen thousand, I guess you got some of mine and some of just about everyone in town. You can see why we got an interest in what goes on, Jim. Yes, sir, we're pullin' for you."

"I never thought of it that way," Martin said. "Looks like I'll have to hurry and pay the bank back so your money'll be safe."

"Yeah," Manners said, and laughed. "When you going to ship, Jim? From what I hear tell, you're fattening up quite a herd." He made a scrubbing motion on the wood with his rag. "It sure is irony, though, that water being on Charlie's place and him never knowing it."

"I brought in that well," Martin said flatly.

"Well, sure you did, Jim," Manners said. "But the water was there. You sure as hell don't expect me to believe you put it there." He tapped the bottle against their glasses. "Come on and have one on the house."

He poured for them and then went on down the bar to find something else to do rather than get into an argument. Martin tossed off his drink, then turned his head as Cal McKitrich came in, beginning his nightly rounds at Manners's saloon. He came up to stand on Martin's right, glanced at the glass Martin held, wiggled his finger.

"Let me have the same." Then he looked at Jim Martin. "Like old times, seeing you two together at the bar." He smiled pleasantly. "You two get your differences settled?"

"What differences?" Martin asked. "Fred and I are the best of friends. Always have been."

"Mmm," McKitrich said and lifted his whiskey. "Well, here's to it lasting."

"You're sure talking funny tonight," Sales said. "I don't make heads or tails of it. You, Jim?"

"No," Martin said. "How about some cards tonight! Say about nine o'clock in my room?"

"That'll be fine," Sales said. "I'll be finished with my chores by then." He clapped Martin on the shoulder and went out.

McKitrich looked after him and, when the doors winnowed, he said: "I like Sales. You ought to let him off the hook, Jim."

"Can't."

"Why not? It was an accident. I'm willing to accept it as that." He took Martin by the arm and led him to a poker table where they could sit down and talk without being overheard. "Jim, I rode over to Rock Springs some time ago, just for a look around. I went out to that old man's place, saw the tree down, and it started me thinking. Now, I don't guess he cut it down, because the people in town said it was standing the day they buried him. Charlie never got to Rock Springs, so he couldn't have cut it down. Which left only you, Jim. That meant it was likely you who met Charlie on the road, got in a beef with him, fought for the gun, and it went off."

"That's the way it happened," Martin said dully. "How come you believe it? You don't really trust anyone, Cal."

"The powder burns on his shirt for one thing," McKitrich said. "One man doesn't pull on another, press the muzzle of the gun against his chest, and shoot." He got up, went to the bar, bought a couple of beers, and brought them back. "Charlie wasn't much, and people knew him as a sour man, full of meanness. Hell, even his wife had a tough time finding enough tears for the funeral. It ain't that you would cause a lot of sadness, Jim. So it must be something else, something that ain't good to keep inside, all locked up."

"Cal, it's my business. I'll take care of it!" He pulled his voice back to softness. "Bess Goddard has done her crying, and talk can't hurt Fred Sales. God damn it, Cal, I'm a busy man, and I can't be bothered with these unimportant trifles."

"Charlie was a man, Jim."

"Hell, you just said he was a no-good."

"Yeah, but he was a man just the same. And you think so too, Jim, or you wouldn't have gone to the trouble to see that folks turned out for his funeral."

Martin regarded him solemnly for a moment, then said: "Cal, did Bess Goddard really write you and ask to come back?"

He sighed, then laughed. "As a matter of fact, she didn't. I wrote to her."

"Then you came to me with that cock-and-bull story? Talked me into taking her and the boy into my house? Why, so they could spy on me and tell you what went on and what was said?"

"No," McKitrich said. "Something meaner than that. I always suspected you, Jim, but you wouldn't say anything. It was my notion that the boy being around all the time would prod you into making a mistake."

"Well, it didn't," Martin said, rising. "Better let this alone, Cal. Now I mean that. It's good enough just the way it is."

McKitrich arched an eyebrow. "Is it? Jim, do you ever find this on your conscience? You know, I wonder because you've always been a man who choked on a lie."

"Men change," Martin said flatly. "So don't spend your time worrying about it."

"Why, I'll let you do that," McKitrich said, surprised as though he believed Martin already knew he would. Martin hesitated, then wheeled, and walked out. After he went down the street, Herb Manners came from around the bar and collected the beer glasses.

"Jim takes himself kind of serious these days, don't he?"

"Wouldn't you?"

211

"I don't know," Manners said. "I never had his prospects." He sat down across from the marshal. "This town's going to see some money one of these days. A boom's been long overdue."

"There's two kinds of boom," McKitrich said. "One of them is an explosion."

"I've never seen either. You know, I'd like to make forty dollars a week out of this place just once, just to see what it was like." He studied the marshal. "You thinking about something I don't know anything about?"

"I'm thinking about water and what it means to a land," McKitrich said. "You ever been a farmer, Herb?"

"Christ, no!"

"Farmers need water more than cattlemen do. And the word will get out about water being found on the prairie. Yes, you can bet on it. Water is news, Herb. The hands will talk about it at the railhead, and the brakie will talk about it in Kansas City, and windmill salesmen will start heading this way with their buggies, and the farmers will be right behind them. I saw this happen in Texas, and in Missouri. You'll get your boom, but it'll be an explosion. Funny about farmers. They're land crazy and, when they see a cattleman owning thirty thousand acres, it makes them fighting mad until they take some of it away from him. Jim Martin ain't thought about this, but he will one of these days, if he's still around."

Manners looked at him, worry in his eyes. "What do you mean, 'if he's still around'? God damn it, Jim's our hope for this town."

"A lot can happen to a big man, especially when he's growing bigger," McKitrich said. He laid a quarter on the poker table, then got up. "Well, I've got rounds to make, Herb, and I want to enjoy it while we still have peace and quiet. Give it some time and there'll be farmers walking the streets in their overalls and hobnailed boots. And I'll move on, if there's any place left for a man to go."

"Don't you ever see the bright side of anything?" Manners asked, a little disgusted. He took the beer glasses to the sink, washed them, and dropped the quarter in the till.

Hansgen was in his office, playing solitaire, when Jim Martin came in and took a chair. Without interrupting his game, Hansgen flipped a telegram across his desk, and Martin read it.

When he laid it down, he said: "Well, the prices are holding low, that's something anyway."

"Better take seven dollars," Hansgen said. "If it goes any lower, you're going to end up in the hole."

"Yes, and if I take seven dollars, I'll make less than half of what I figured." He bit off the end of a cigar and thought about his problem while he searched for a match.

Hansgen raked one across his desk and leaned forward with it. After he whipped it out, he said: "Jim, you don't have much choice. There's only one other, and I wouldn't risk it."

"Holding the herd until prices come up?" Martin shrugged. "I can go six months. It's worth it to me."

His tone made Hansgen forget his game. "You damned fool, don't do a thing like that! Jesus, do you expect Kinred to float you?"

"Another six thousand won't kill him."

"No, but it'll leave him strapped and bankrupt if the prices plunge." He brushed the cards into a careless pile and leaned his elbows on the table. "Jim, you're land poor, and you've got water, but even that isn't worth much if cattle prices are down to rock bottom. Your house isn't worth a nickel on the market because no one would want that eye-sore."

"Eye-sore?" Martin said angrily. "That's a beautiful house."

"All right, all right, I didn't mean to insult you," Hansgen said. "I just don't want you doing something stupid." He took out his sack of makings and rolled a smoke. "Jim, you know what a stock speculator is. He'll buy when the market is shaky and gamble that it will rise, and if it goes bust, then he'll cover the losses with other investments. Well, that's what you're doing, but all your eggs are in one basket and, if the market price of beef slides, you'll disappear for good. Now, let me sell for you. I can send a wire tonight, sell them at closing prices, and promise delivery in thirty days. Take your smaller profit and wait and then, if the market skids to hell, buy heavy for practically nothing and wait for the rise. You'd make a higher margin of profit then."

"I paid four and a half for the stock," Martin said. "If I sell for seven now, that's only two and a half dollars' profit."

"So?"

"So, suppose the market rises and I have to buy for six, or eight? What do I buy with?"

"A loan," Hansgen said. "Jim, selling now at seven would clear you and get Kinred off the hook. He's overextended himself. With everything clear you could buy for eight and ride a higher market."

"I like my profit big and quick," Martin said. "And if I have to gamble, I'll do it on what I have today, not what

214

I might have tomorrow." He knocked ash off his cigar. "The market's been hanging low but steady. I don't think it'll go lower."

"Jim, if this was your money you were playing with, I'd say to do as you damned please. But it isn't your money. It's the bank's and belongs to every depositor in this town. Go slow, Jim. Don't be in such a rush to make it. Why can't you be like Fred Sales?"

"Maybe I wouldn't want to be like him," Martin said. "It's all right for him to be slow and cautious. He's an older man who could never make it up if he really lost. I can't lose. When I dug my first well, I said I'd get water, and I did. And I said I'd get water when I sank this last well. Everything I've said has been so. Now, I say that the market isn't going any lower, and I'm holding my stock until it rises."

Hansgen stared at him. "Jim, you just said that as though it wouldn't dare go lower."

"Maybe that's it," Martin said flatly. "A man can have strange powers sometimes . . . powers he hasn't fully explored yet . . . and I'm sure I'm right."

"Well," Hansgen said, sighing, "I'm a cattle buyer not a business advisor. And you're the kind of man who'll always do what he wants in spite of what everyone else says. But don't you think you ought to talk this over with Kinred first? I mean, he'll have to loan you money now to tide you over and. . . ."

"And what?" Martin asked. "Kinred's in with me all the way. If he's nervous, then he'll have to get over it. If he doesn't know what he's doing, then he'll have to believe that I do."

"Yeah. Well, you've been right so far. I sure hope you are this time for everybody's sake."

# Chapter Twenty-One

This was the hottest July anyone remembered, with the thermometer hanging in the hundred-and-seven region when the sun was highest, and dropping to the relatively cool nineties at night. It was cruel heat for a man to work in, and because of this Jim Martin kept his hands as idle as possible. They did most of their work in the early morning hours and after the sun had set.

Each day a man rode to town and back and brought the latest market report. Beef prices continued to remain low, holding there, just as Martin had predicted they would. And twice during July Martin drove to town to talk to Kinred at the bank for he had a payroll to meet and other expenses.

August brought no break in the weather. The glassy sun and pale sky continued, and a bake-oven heat was everywhere, turning the prairie into a parched wasteland. The creek merely trickled over the spillway, and with each night wind Martin's windmills pumped furiously to bring up enough water to last through the next day.

Life was a nip-and-tuck existence, and Martin decided that, as soon as he shipped and cleared his debts, he was going to buy two small steam engines and pump water with them. The wind was too unreliable.

Hansgen was beginning to change his mind about his prophesy on how far he expected beef prices to drop. It seemed that they had finally leveled off low and would stay there a while before coming up. At least he no longer worried about Martin's decision to hold his herd for a rise in prices. And the depositors of Morgan Tanks lost their first fears and grimly hung on, feeling that any time now the break would come, and the waiting would be over.

Martin wasn't sure what he wanted first, a break in the prices or a break in the heat. He had never known either to remain static for so long. Several times he had decided to ride over and see how Fred Sales was making out, but the heat made him listless, and he stayed around the house, waiting and feeling powerless to do anything else. Martin was irritated, annoyed at his inability to alter his situation. He disliked being at the mercy of Chicago-made prices and God-made heat.

The change came late at night. He knew nothing of it until Tip came to the house and found him alone in the parlor. Martin was just finishing his last cigar before retiring, and he looked around when Tip knocked lightly, politely on the door frame.

"Yes?" Martin said.

"The well's stopped pumping," Tip said.

Panic was a flood in his chest, but he stemmed it and spoke calmly. "Nonsense. Something's wrong with the suction." He butted out his cigar and went out with Tip, closing the outside screen door quietly so as not to disturb anyone.

Tip had already rigged a lantern in the windmill framing. It cast a yellow glow around the pump rod, still moving slowly up and down but drawing no water. Martin shut off the pump and, after Tip brought some tools from the shed, he began to disassemble the pump. He worked for hours, trying to hurry, yet trying to be careful, to make no mistakes, and all the time wondering if his mistakes hadn't been made some time ago.

217

He had some jabs of suspicion that cutting down the tree had something to do with this, and he told himself not to be ridiculous. There was a purely mechanical reason why the water stopped, and he would find it.

Daylight began to crowd back the night before he would admit that there was nothing wrong with the pump. He took it to the huge water tanks and tested it, and it pumped perfectly.

"I guess the well's dry, Mister Martin," Tip said.

Martin almost hit him but checked himself in time. "We don't know that!"

"It sure ain't givin' water." He shifted his feet. "You want me for anything else?"

"No," Martin said. "There's enough water in the tanks for another day. I want the cattle kept in this section moved over to the sink. That well's still strong."

"Yes, sir. What you going to do, Mister Martin?"

"Send for the driller and find out what's happened!" Martin said. "And drill another well if I have to."

He had to go to town to send a telegram, and he had to tell Jennifer why he was going to town. After he sent the telegram, the whole town would know that his well had turned off dry. Well, none of it could be helped. If they panicked, there wasn't much he could do about it, but he wasn't going to panic himself. This was a time when a man needed his head and his courage.

Jennifer surprised him by taking the news calmly, as though she had expected it to happen for some time. He did not understand this, and it made him angry, her reasoning that a man had just so much luck and that he had run out of his. That was a fool woman's logic all right. She'd probably sit right down and read the Bible.

On the way to town he had to fight against a pushing sense of haste. There was something terribly wrong. He couldn't wait to get it fixed, and he was certain that it could be fixed. In a way he dreaded telling Kinred about the dry well. The man was so damned conservative and easily frightened that Martin felt a little sorry for him. He always thought that a banker ought to be a little more daring.

Kinred said nothing when Martin told him, just reached into his desk drawer for a bottle and a glass, and Martin left the bank, not wanting to watch a man get drunk. He sent his telegram and drove home to wait. With a good team and a buggy the driller ought to arrive day after tomorrow. A day to fix the pump, or the well, or whatever was wrong, and Martin could laugh about the whole damn thing. And Jennifer would feel foolish and Kinred a little ashamed for cracking so easily, but Martin knew he could forget all that.

While he waited for the driller, Martin spent a good deal of time at the sink. He told himself that he wanted to see how his cattle were making out with one well, whether there'd be enough water, but he kept watching the well, wondering in spite of himself whether it would give out like the other one. With both wells pumping, being overstocked was bad, but with only one well left the situation was almost intolerable. He decided to contact Hansgen the latter part of the week and sell off part of his herd even if the driller fixed the other well. This was Martin's first admission that he was working close to the wire, and he thought of it as an acknowledgment of weakness rather than as any facing of the facts.

The driller arrived in the early evening and immediately

inspected the well. His decision was quick, sure. "She's dry."

"It can't be dry," Martin said.

"She is dry," the driller said. "Way I figure it is that this bed of sandstone runs on a slant from here to the sink. We had to go deeper for water there, you recall. I think we've drained this pool dry."

"You mean this well is finished?"

"No, no, I didn't say that. More than likely there's a bigger pool under this dry one. It's only a matter of drilling deeper." He pushed his hat forward and scratched the back of his head. "You want I should bring up a rig and start drilling?"

"I'll have to talk to my banker first," Martin said. "Maybe you'd like to come to town with me in the morning."

"Sure," the driller said. "Be obliged to, Mister Martin."

"How long will that other well last?"

"Can't say. May never go dry because of seepage into the sandstone layer. Then, too, it may only be a winter well and go dry every summer. There are wells like that, Mister Martin."

"I've got to have water all year around," Martin said. He took the man by the arm and led him to the house. Bess Goddard saw that he was given a room, and Martin went into the library and closed the doors.

He tried to project Kinred's reaction to a request for more money. The man would resist, argue, and say no, but Martin was certain that Kinred would in the end give in and pay for another well. What else could he do? If he refused, called in the notes, he'd lose everything. Martin felt secure in his position — secure and very shaken at the same time — and

220

it gave him more than a little concern.

It was Martin's observation that a banker liked to have a good cigar between his fingers before he talked business. They sat in Kinred's office, and Martin watched him light his cigar.

Kinred asked the questions. "How much would it cost to drill into the main pool?"

"About eight hundred dollars," the driller said. "I've run into this a hundred times. All through Illinois and Iowa and them states it's like that. Of course, you get your water without going so deep because the Saint Peter's sandstone comes close to the surface there." The driller shook his head and smiled as though amused. "It's a funny thing about the drillin' business, Mister Kinred. Been at it almost thirty years, and my father before me. Back among the farmers they don't think a thing about goin' two hundred feet for a strong pool. But I guess that's because they've always relied on a well. When I came out here, I figured I'd be diggin' a lot of wells because cattle need water. It ain't so. Cattlemen are used to gettin' their water from a creek or river. They can't believe you can sink a pipe and get it. Well, a farmer ain't got a thing against a creek or a river, but creeks dry up and rivers change course, but a well keeps right on giving up water, if you drill to the main pool."

"And you think eight hundred dollars will do the job?"

"Yes, sir. I'd guarantee water at no more than that cost."

Kinred leaned back and puffed his cigar. "With a good well that land would support a farmer, wouldn't it?"

"Oh, sure," the driller said. "A man could put a well down almost any place and get water. You see, that sandstone streak runs all through that side of the creek. Some sections of country is like that, Mister Kinred. You can sink a well most any place."

"Is that why Sales brought in two dry holes?"

"My, no! You got to witch for water over there. Sales wanted the well drilled where he'd decided it should be. Can't get water that way."

"All right," Kinred said. "Go sink the well and come to me when you're through. I'll have your money for you."

"Well, it's Mister Martin's place and. . . ."

"You just come here. I'll pay you." He got up, showed him the way out, then came back to his desk.

"You could have credited my account," Martin said. "What were you trying to do, make me look foolish?"

"I've put the last nickel I'm going to into your place," Kinred said. "You've gone out too far, Jim. Pull in now and redeem your notes, or I'll foreclose."

Martin straightened in the chair. "What was that?"

"You heard me. I'm calling in your notes in thirty days. You're not a sane gambler, Jim. A gambler knows that he can lose, but you don't."

"So you're going to break me," Martin said. He leaned back in his chair and smiled. "Kinred, you're trying to bluff me down. If you take my place, what would you do with it? No, you're not going to close me out."

"You have thirty days in which to find out," Kinred said flatly. He looked steadily at Martin, then shook his head. "You don't understand this at all, do you, Jim?"

"No. I think it's a low deal to get what I've worked so hard to build." He got up and turned to the door, stopping there. "When you send McKitrich to throw me off, tell him to bring help. He's going to need it."

"I imagine he'll be able to find it," Kinred said.

On the walk Martin had to pause to gather himself. He was so angry that his hands trembled. So that was the way the game was played? Let a man get way out on the limb and chop it off. By God, no man would do that with him.

With long strides he went down the street to Hansgen's office. The cattle buyer was reading a Chicago newspaper, and he put it aside when Martin came in. "The same," he said. "Like the heat, you think the damn stuff will never go away."

"I want to sell," Martin said.

Hansgen took his feet off the desk and stared. "Why the switch?"

"It doesn't matter. I want to sell and ship."

"Weeeelll, the picture has changed a little, Jim. The speculators have backed off now. You'll have to sell to a packer in Kansas City and at the market price when they arrive and are tallied. You want to take that big of a gamble?" He made some mental calculations. "Take you five days to gather, six to drive to the railroad, and three-four more to get there. That's damned near two weeks, and once your stock is loaded, it's up to God and the market as to how you'll come out."

"I want to sell," Jim Martin said.

Hansgen sighed. "I'll get the telegram off in an hour." He offered Martin his hand. "The best of luck, Jim."

"Thanks," Martin said and went out to find the driller.

They did not talk during the ride home, and Martin gave his buggy and team to one of the hands to put away. Then he found Tip and told him that they were to round up every head of stock on the place and be ready to drive in five days. It was a big order, but Tip was used to big orders. He just nodded and got busy.

Going into the house, Martin went up the winding stairs to the second floor and on up to the third. The guest rooms were in the rear wing, and he stopped at a door and knocked.

When it opened, a dark-haired, mustached man smiled. "Mister Martin, what a pleasure to meet you." He stepped aside. "Come in, please." He swept some soiled shirts off a chair so Martin could sit down. "I have seen you about the ranch, but unfortunately we have never found time to meet. What can I do for you?"

"I've been thinking about you all the way home," Martin said.

"Oh? How flattering," he said.

"Not flattering, Mister Barsotti. I thought, here's a man, living in my house for months, hired by my wife, and I've never even taken the time to meet him. I don't even know if I like him or approve of him."

"I can assure you my references are the. . . ."

"I'm sure they are," Martin said quickly. "You're missing my point, Mister Barsotti, or perhaps I don't have a point to make. I came here to tell you that I could no longer afford you."

"You mean I'm discharged?" He sounded horrified.

"Yes. You're a luxury, Mister Barsotti, and you're here because I wanted luxuries just because I'd never had any before. My wife will give you two weeks' pay."

When Martin got up, Barsotti all but barred his way to the door. "Have I offended you? Have I failed . . . ?"

"Nothing like that," Martin said softly. "I just can't afford you. Good night."

He went out, closed the door, and went down the stairs, thinking how incredible it was for the man to have been in this huge house all this time without having met him.

Then, again, it wasn't incredible at all for this was the first time Martin had ever gone to the third floor, and for that matter he wasn't even aware of what furniture filled each of the rooms. It had all been selected by a firm in Kansas City.

He had a moment of rare insight and realized that much of his living now was strange to him. He had been moving in unreality and had convinced himself that he liked it. Fortune had brought him no closer to anything, and perhaps it had pushed him farther away from the things he had once known to be true. Certainly it had pushed him away from himself until knowledge of himself was lost. In his mind he tried to determine the basic truth, why he was determined to fight now to retain what he had when it obviously meant little to him. When he had money, he spent it. It had no particular value to him. This house, ten times larger than he needed, was built to impress everyone, and once they were impressed, he might as well have torn it down for it served no further function. He decided to go a step further and assume that now that he had risen from rags to importance, he could go back to rags without particular regret, for he had established his ability to do it. Then he understood why some men took pride in saying that they had won and lost several fortunes. Just having it once elevated a man so that no real poverty thereafter could take away the shine, the importance of once having been somebody.

Jennifer was in the parlor with the boys, playing a game with them, and she left them as soon as Martin came into the room. "I just told Mister Barsotti that we can no longer employ him," Martin said. He took out a cigar and bent toward the lamp for his light. "Kinred wants me to pay off the notes in thirty days, so I'm selling off the entire herd."

"Are we broke, Jim?"

He shrugged. "In cash, pretty close." He reached into his pocket and counted what he had. "Three hundred and eighty dollars."

"I have nearly two hundred," she said. Then she suddenly put her arms around him and hugged him. "Within sixty dollars, that's what we started out with, Jim."

He held her and found comfort in her. "Yes, it wasn't much." Then he patted her back and released her. "If the market holds, I can spit in Kinred's eye. Of course, after the notes are paid off, there won't be much left. But the place will still be ours, and we can slowly build back a herd."

"Jim, let's sit down and talk." She took his arm, led him to a chair, then sat on the rug beside him. "What are we really losing? Have you asked yourself that?"

"I haven't lost yet," he said, "and I don't want to lose." He let his eyes pull nearly shut and puffed gently on his cigar. "All my life I've wanted to be an important man. I am important, Jennifer. And I can never really give up a thing. It's the way I am. Not long ago you said my luck was running out, that I'd wasted what I had. You may be right but, when the last of it is gone, I'll still be here, still trying to change it, make it different. The market's shot, and one well has dried up, and Kinred wants his money back, but I'm not licked. Not by a damn jugful I'm not licked."

Jennifer remained quiet for a moment, then said: "Jim, I've learned something from this. Hard luck wipes out a big man just as easily as it wipes out a little one. The only difference is, where the little man doesn't have much to lose, the big man has more chances to lose it. The broom sweeps the same, Jim, whether it's a little pile or a big one."

"You don't really care, do you?"

"Yes, I care because being poor again wouldn't bring you back to me the way you once were. We've changed, and we won't change back, so it is a loss. But don't be afraid of losing, Jim. There's nothing unmanly about it."

# Chapter Twenty-Two

Every time Jim Martin saw the tree lying amid a tangle of broken branches and dead leaves, he was pulled back to that time when his faith was strong, and he had prayed for a saving rain, and he had admitted to himself that God gave, and God took away. The tree reminded him that he had lost faith, reminded him that his vanity and pride made him take credit for something divine in nature and, because the tree affected him this way, Martin ordered it bucked up into fireplace logs and put behind the woodshed in ricks.

He busied himself with the details of the gather. They were going to start the drive in two days, and the drilling rig arrived and a crew, and a deeper hole was being sunk. Yet the whole thing had a theatrical air to it, like some general lining up his soldiers so they could all be shot down when the battle began.

Fred Sales came over. He was a man sensitive to the troubles of others. Sales didn't say much about shipping on Hansgen's terms, or the well going dry, or Kinred's pending foreclosure, or how much the people in Morgan Tanks were going to suffer if the bank had to close. He acted as though these things couldn't make much difference, but Jim Martin knew they could. And that was why Martin had to win. He couldn't bear to think of himself as the cause of it all or the cause of anything. It wasn't his rôle in life to create events. He only endured the events created by others. Somehow this became mixed up with him, and the things he did affected so many people he couldn't keep track of it all.

"Kinred isn't fooling me," Martin said to Sales. "He's going to take my land and sell it to farmers. I can see the scheme in his mind. You don't want farmers across the creek from you, Fred."

"I could live with it," Sales said. "Rather have you, though, Jim. Always rather have a man I know and trust."

Martin felt a thrust of shame for he didn't deserve this from Sales, and he understood that he would probably feel this way the rest of his life every time Sales offered his friendship. "Do you believe in luck, Fred?"

"Sure. Once a man has had his share of the bad and a taste of the good, he can't help but believe in it."

"I heard an interesting idea," Martin said. "Herb's pet theory."

"How's that?"

"That there's just so much luck in the world. You can't create it or destroy it. So, when one man comes into some good luck, someone else has to give up a little."

"It kind of makes sense, don't it? Now, take yourself. A year ago I was making out good, Charlie Goddard, fair, and you, poorly. Then Charlie started to lose a little of his luck, and you got it, and the more Charlie lost, the more you got. Then mine began to go sour, and you got that too. I guess it started to level off when Charlie got himself killed. That's about the worst luck a man can have. Mine sort of leveled off, Jim. Me and Edith had never got along, you know, and many a time I expected her to up and leave. But there wasn't any money. And after we let the men go, we had to work three times as hard. I thought Edith would leave me sure then, but, by golly, she dug right in, and we fell in love all over again. She's goin' to have a baby in the spring."

"The hell you say!"

Sales grinned and nodded. "Right then I knew some of my luck was coming back, and it has slow but sure. But, now, I can see how you had to lose some so I could have it."

"Someone else has been getting a share," Martin said. "I've got damned little left."

They talked a while longer, then Sales rode home, and Martin went into the house. As soon as the cattle money arrived, Martin was going to pay off the servants and let them go, including Bess Goddard. He hated to think of that, but he had no choice. She would have to make do for herself. Many times now he had meant to get her aside and tell her what really happened that night on the road, just so she'd know. The boy would want to know, too, even though he had stopped blaming Jim Martin, stopped accusing him with his eyes. But Martin held the knowledge within himself, and he knew now that it was too late to say anything, and he supposed Bess and the boy had really stopped caring one way or another.

Thursday evening, two days after Tip and the crew left the ranch to drive to the railhead, Tad came in from the sink and told his father that the well had gone dry. The sink was full of water still, and the surrounding grazing land was still green from the irrigating, but it wouldn't stay that way. Martin nodded, that was all, and he couldn't decide whether he had expected this or not. Somehow it fit a pattern that he had himself established, and he thought of it as a painful justice for his rude slashing of the earth to bleed her quickly dry. All he could hope for now was for the driller to break through and raise water. The fact that he could only hope, rather than believe as the driller believed, caused him a moment of hesitation. Once, when old man Patchin had told him about the tree, Martin had believed it. The driller was as certain as Patchin had been, but Martin no longer had faith in the words of another man.

He knew what Jennifer thought, that he had sinned and was now paying for it. Martin didn't believe that either, yet he couldn't get the notion out of his head. He should have taken it as a sign when the trees around the sink died and never drilled that well. And he knew that he should never have cut the tree down and defied powers a lot stronger than himself. But he had done these things because he thought he could stand alone, do it alone. Now he wondered if that hadn't been a delusion designed to trap him.

All this bad luck meant something. Men were not crushed by fate as a meaningless gesture. He only wanted a sign, just a small sign that he was not completely dropped from favor. A little thing like that could do a lot to restore a man's confidence.

At night the driller's rig kept him awake; so much depended on the well. Then early one morning the steam engine stopped, and he got out of bed to see what caused this delay. Lanterns were hanging on the rig, and the driller was there, grinning, his hands and face muddy.

"I said she'd come in, didn't I?" He laughed. "Fifty-two feet I went for the main pool. You got your water, Mister Martin, and this one won't dry up on you."

"Thank God," Martin said and returned to the house. Jennifer was up, tying her robe tightly about her. "The well's in," he said, meeting her in the upper hallway.

231

"We're all right now. Everything's all right." He put his arms around her, held her, and kissed her. "It'll be nip and tuck this next year, but with the water we'll be all right."

"It was there all the time, only you didn't drill deep enough?"

"Yes. All the years we spit dust and hauled water, it was under our feet, just waiting for a drill to go down and get it."

"Don't forget what led you to drill for it," Jennifer said.

"The tree?" He turned serious. "Yes. I wish I hadn't cut it down now. I haven't felt good about it since. Damn a man's pride, his fool notions!" With his arm around her he turned her into the huge bedroom and closed the door. "Kinred's going to scream when he hears we got water because he's planning on foreclosing, taking this place over and selling it to farmers. Well, I'll beat him, Jennifer. I'll beat him good, and one of these days I'll buy his damned bank and turn it into a dance hall. I'll let him sell tickets."

"The dreams have never really left your mind at all, have they?"

He looked at her as though he had only half heard her. "What are you talking about?"

"I'm talking about you," she said softly. "Jim, at supper you were a man with his back to the wall, a realistic man who was trying to survive with his dignity. There were no grand schemes then, just a hope that life wouldn't kick you too hard. Now you've got a well, it's all changed. All changed back to growing and getting bigger and remembering all the slights so you can step on them where it hurts."

"Do you think he'd show me any mercy?"

"Probably he wouldn't," she said. "What does it matter, Jim? What does it really matter?"

He got up and walked about the room. "It matters that I can't have people think they can trick me and get away with it. I'm going into town tomorrow and see Kinred. We'll have it out. As soon as I get my cattle check, I'll pay him off and be through with him."

"Why don't you think about it first?"

"Hell, I have thought about it. I've thought about it since Kinred pulled the foreclosure notice on me. Well, it didn't work, Jennifer." He took her arms and looked into her eyes, turning her so that the lamplight fell on her face. "You always worried about the land beating a man down, crushing him, draining him until there wasn't anything left but a short funeral and a wooden headstone. That's not my lot, Jennifer. Can't you see that I was born to beat the land? I'll make no mistakes now, girl. You can bet on it. It's Kinred who has made the mistake. He's the one who'll be beaten." He laughed softly and slapped his stomach, feeling good about his prospects now. "The land is like a mean horse. You've got to watch it all the time because it's full of tricks and a man only has one chance. Well, I know all the tricks, old girl. I'm not going to do anything foolish. Kinred and I'll have a talk, and I'll tell him he's been whipped, and I'll come home. Now, there's nothing to fear in that, is there?"

"You've played enough cards to know about an ace in the hole," she said seriously.

"What can he do? The only weapon he has is the notes I signed and, when I redeem them, he's no longer running anything."

"I want to go in with you in the morning," Jennifer said.

He was amused at her concern. "All right, if it will make you feel any better."

"It will," she said. "Jim, you've had a lot go bad for you, and I wouldn't want to see anything more go the same way. It might be too much to take."

"You think I'd break? Come on, go back to bed. You're talking nonsense."

They had breakfast early and were on the road before the sun was fully up. Martin took advantage of the coolness to drive fast, making good time into town. He arrived with the day's strong heat, stabled the team, and went with Jennifer along the board walk. She had some shopping to do, and he left her at the store, then cut across to the bank.

Kinred was at his desk, and he smiled when Martin came in. "I've been thinking about driving out to your place, but it's been too blamed hot. Get your water?"

"Yes," Martin said. "And I came in to talk to you about it." A wagon came down the street, and he turned his head to see who it was. He did not recognize the man at all. The man's family was in the back of the wagon, four children and a large tan dog. "Who the hell was that?"

"I don't know," Kinred said vaguely. "So you got your well?"

"That's right. And I'll be getting my cattle check soon, so I'll clear off those notes." He watched Kinred, expecting to see surprise, perhaps disappointment. Only there was none of these things.

"Well, you shouldn't worry about it," Kinred said. "I'm not."

"Who the hell's worried, anyway? I just didn't like the sly way you did business. And when I'm clear, I'll be banking somewhere else."

"Jim, stop dreaming. You're never going to get clear."

"What?" Martin said it as though he hadn't heard right.

"I said you're not getting clear, now or ever. That fella you saw go by in the wagon with his family, he's a farmer. There's nine more families in town, Jim. I've cut up your place, sold it. It's just a formality now of transferring the papers."

"You can't sell something I own!"

Kinred smiled. "Jim, in another week you won't own it. There isn't going to be any cattle check." He saw the flatness go into Martin's eyes and quickly opened a desk drawer, putting his hand on a revolver there. "You want me to explain it to you?"

"You'd better," Martin said tightly.

"Go talk to Hansgen, then. Jim, three days before I talked to you, cattle prices nose dived. I knew I could force you to sell, but I didn't want you to sell when there was a chance of your breaking anywhere even. So Hansgen and I agreed to wait until the prices fell, then let you think they still held. I'd force you to sell, and you'd come out so far in debt that you'd never get out."

Martin half lunged at Kinred and stopped, for the banker pulled the pistol from the drawer and cocked it.

"Now, you don't want me to shoot you, do you, Jim?"

"You god-damned crook!" Martin said. "You sit here on your fat ass while I eat dust and break my back making something so you can take it away from me!"

"It's life," Kinred said. "Now, you'd better get out of

here quietly before I have to use this or call McKitrich. I'm in the right, you know. You'd never be able to prove a thing against me, Jim."

"I'm going to get a gun," Martin said softly, "and I'm going to kill Hansgen, then come back and kill you."

"All right, you do that." He held the gun until Jim Martin went out.

Leaning against the bank wall, Jim closed his eyes and tried to still his fury. He jumped slightly when Cal McKitrich spoke at his elbow.

"The axe fell, huh, Jim?"

Martin looked at him. "You knew, huh?"

"No, I didn't know. It's on your face. Better cool off."

"You seen Hansgen?"

"In his office. Why?"

"I'm going to shoot him, that's why. I've lost my place, Cal. Lost everything."

"And now you want to lose your life?" The marshal shook his head. "Jim, Hansgen is a Texan. Remember, he came north with a herd, and he can handle a gun."

"That doesn't scare me."

"Christ, I'm not saying you're scared. Just get smart. You want to throw your life away? Think of your wife, man. Your boy." He took Martin by the sleeve and pulled him a little closer. "Jim, I told you once that a big man was a target for every little man. So don't be so damned surprised, so hurt because you forgot about it, and someone else didn't. You shoot Hansgen, you won't solve a damned thing. He'll leave all the gravy for Kinred. Do you want him to cut your place up into little chunks and sell it to the farmers?"

"He's already done that," Martin said. "Are you blind? Haven't you seen 'em with their wagons?"

"Yeah, I saw 'em," McKitrich said. "But I don't care about them, Jim. Possession is nine points of the law."

"Yes, and Kinred will have to kill me to get me off my place!"

"You damned fool, don't think he isn't working on it. Look at yourself, all worked up into a mad to go after Hansgen. Why, you're like a piece of clay in Kinred's hands, doin' everything he wants you to do. Go ahead and fight Hansgen, and if you win, then you've done Kinred a favor. He won't have to pay Hansgen for helping him. And if Hansgen gets you, Kinred got the job done cheaply enough." He looked into Martin's eyes. "The thing that gets you, Jim, is that you never did consider Kinred much of anything. I'll bet you've never really looked at him. What color eyes has he got? What's his first name? You don't know. Well, that was a mistake, Jim, because by not noticing him, you left the door open for him to sneak in and knife you."

"I made the mistake," Martin said. "I admit it, but I can also correct it."

"Not this one and you know it," McKitrich said. "All there is to do, Jim, is to satisfy your desire for revenge. God damn it, so you've been beaten. You're not the first man who's gone broke out here. Why court a fight that could leave you dead? Be a little smarter than the last man and just be money broke, not dead broke."

"You make a hell of a good speech," Martin said. "Unfortunately, it don't help a damned bit. I've been sold out by two sharp operators, and now I'm going to spill a little blood over it."

McKitrich sighed and pawed his mouth out of shape. "Your wife and boy don't count, huh? They go through this with you, but you're the only one who's hurt, huh?

Hell, I can't talk to you any more."

He turned and walked across the street to the store where Martin's wife stood on the porch. There was worry in the lines of her face, and she spoke as McKitrich came up. "Something's wrong. Why is Jim standing over there like that?"

McKitrich took her arm and steered her inside and to one side so he could talk. "Where's the boy?"

"At home. Cal, what's wrong?"

He told her and watched her carefully, thinking that she would break at the news, but she didn't. She took it better than her husband. "Just how much is there left for us?" she asked.

"The clothes on your back," McKitrich said. "Everything else is pack and parcel and included in Kinred's fore-closure." He glanced out the window and saw Martin still leaning against the bank wall. "Do you want me to fetch Jim over, get him out of town? If I keep talking to him, I might be able to make him see sense and just ride out. There isn't anything else he can do." He patted Jennifer's arm. "Wait here. I'll go fetch him."

He crossed the street, got Martin to come back with him and, when Martin saw Jennifer, he acted terribly ashamed and wouldn't look at her, as though this were all his fault and that he had disgraced himself. Jennifer put her arm around him and said: "Jim, it's all right. It really is. We can start again."

Martin looked at her, a little amazed that she could suggest such a thing, for he'd come all the way up from the bottom and hit the top, and now he was on the bottom again, and the ride had been a dizzy one, and he wasn't very sorry about much of any of it, except that it made his prospects for tomorrow seem terribly dull.

"You really want to start over?" he asked. "You really could?"

"Yes," Jennifer said. "Jim, take the licking . . . it won't kill you to do it."

He shook his head, unable to bring himself to this state of mind, where he could acknowledge the totality of his defeat and take a new momentum in a forward direction. "I'd hate to disappoint Hansgen," Martin said. "If I did that to a man and afterward he didn't come to me with his fight, I'd be a little disappointed." He looked at McKitrich. "She doesn't understand, Cal. She doesn't know how good it feels to put a man down after he's hurt you. Hansgen's got to pay. He expects to pay."

Martin turned and walked over to the counter, and Jennifer would have followed him except that McKitrich held her back. "Let him go," he said and stood there while Martin bought a walnut-handled .44 and a box of shells. He stood at the counter, loaded the gun, held it in his hand.

Then he came back to where his wife and McKitrich waited. He said to her: "This must seem useless to you, and in a way, I imagine, it is, hitting back at a man just because he wanted something you had. I guess it isn't that either, but what they've done is showed everybody that I've been all I can ever be, and now I'm where I ought to be, cleaning out somebody's barn or working on a manure pile." He hefted the gun. "So I just got to shoot Hansgen and let everyone know they can't do this to me."

He started to turn away and, when his back was to them, McKitrich smoothly drew his pistol and brought the barrel crashing down on Jim Martin's head. Then he caught him before he fell and held him. Jennifer gasped and stared at her unconscious husband.

"I shouldn't have done that," McKitrich said. "I should have let him get himself killed. You know, Hansgen is Texan, and he'd shoot Jim before he got his gun cocked. No, I got to do him this favor and keep him alive. Son of a gun, he reached for the sky and touched it, didn't he? All the way up from the dust, he reached up and touched his own kind of heaven, and a man ought to go on living after that just for the pure pleasure of remembering. Now, you go get the buggy and we'll load him in. And don't worry about when he comes around. He won't come back to cause trouble. And don't you worry none about him. He'll get along. You just see that he goes over to Sales and gets a job. He'll cuss and hate to ask, but Jim's a damned practical man once he gets it figured out where his place is. Now go on, get the buggy. I'll wait here with him."

He lowered Martin to the floor, then stood by the window, looking at the dingy street. A cluster of farmers, all strangers to Morgan Tanks, had their wagons parked near the bank. Kinred was there, talking to them, waiting to see how much trouble Jim Martin would give him.

Then Jennifer came back with the buggy, and McKitrich carried Martin outside and put him in, pushing him in the corner so he wouldn't fall out. Kinred saw it, and down the street Hansgen saw it, and everyone knew that Martin's chance for squaring accounts had passed. The next time he came to town the privilege to take this up was no longer his. McKitrich knew that this was a tremendous decision to be making for another man, yet he had made it without hesitation, and he

240

hoped that some day Martin would understand why and forgive him for it.

Jennifer was getting into the buggy, picking up the reins. "I know he'll be all right, Marshal." She smiled. "Poor Jim, he wasn't cut out to be too big a man. It just got too much for him. It's too bad we couldn't have saved some of it, just a little of it for him to start over with."

"Some never do," McKitrich said softly. "Jim's the win all, lose all kind." Then he stepped back and raised a hand to the brim of his hat, and Jennifer wheeled the team out of town.

Kinred was still standing by the bank, talking earnestly to the farmers, and they listened carefully. McKitrich could imagine what Kinred was saying for it had been said before by the first man who had wanted to sell his five sections of dust. He would be telling them about how rich the earth was and how nice it would plow and all a man had to do to get a crop to grow would be to pour a little water on it — and a little of his blood and youth — and to save a little patch in which to bury him. . . . McKitrich felt like rushing across the street to the farmers and telling them the truth, but he held himself back, knowing they wouldn't believe him. They would go out there, fence their sections, spend their money to have wells drilled, and perhaps they'd make it, and perhaps they wouldn't and that would be too bad, yet there was something glorious in a man's effort, especially when he made a big effort like Jim Martin had.

That was why, McKitrich decided, that he'd knocked Martin out to keep him from getting himself killed. He wanted to save him, sort of as a reward for the try he'd made. It was a good try, a clean try, or about as clean as any man was expected to make, considering the

241

enormity of his ambition. No, Martin didn't have much to be ashamed of, and he'd realize that. And who knows? Maybe he'd try again. Some men did. It was something pleasant for McKitrich to think about.

## THE END

**Will Cook** is the author of numerous outstanding Western novels as well as historical frontier fiction. He was born in Richmond, Indiana, but was raised by an aunt and uncle in Cambridge, Illinois. He joined the U.S. cavalry at the age of sixteen but was disillusioned because horses were being eliminated through mechanization. He transferred to the U.S. Army Air Force in which he served in the South Pacific during the Second World War. Cook turned to writing in 1951 and contributed a number of outstanding short stories to *Dime Western* and other pulp magazines as well as fiction for major smooth-paper magazines such as *The Saturday Evening Post*. It was in the *Post* that his best-known novel *Comanche Captives* was serialized. It was later filmed as *Two Rode Together* (Columbia, 1961) directed by John Ford and starring James Stewart and Richard Widmark. Sometimes in his short stories Cook would introduce characters that would later be featured in novels, such as Charlie Boomhauer who first appeared in *Lawmen Die Sudden* in *Big-Book Western* in 1953 and is later to be found in *Badman's Holiday* (1958) and *The Wind River Kid* (1958). Along with his steady productivity, Cook maintained an enviable quality. His novels range widely in time and place, from the Illinois frontier of 1811 to southwest Texas in 1905, but each is peopled with credible and interesting characters whose interactions form the backbone of the narrative. Most of his novels deal with more or less traditional Western themes—range wars, reformed outlaws, cattle rustling, Indian fighting—but there are also romantic novels such as *Sabrina Kane* (1956) and exercises in historical realism such as *Elizabeth, by Name* (1958). Indeed, his fiction is known for its strong heroines. Another common feature is Cook's compassion for his characters who must be able to survive in a wild and violent land. His protagonists made mistakes, hurt people they care for, and sometimes succumb to ignoble impulses, but this all provides an added dimension to the artistry of his work.